# Ken Lansdowne

## Daily ☉ Chronicle

# BATHHOUSE BLOODBATH!

hui etryhop etryhop etryhop etryhop etryhop
dfh edrthyr edrthyrij edrthyr edrthyr edrthyr
uiy ijhkl;;x hkl;;xmx ijhkl;;x ijhkl;;x ijhkl;;x
hhu mxhxdl hxdl;d;[f mxhxdl mxhxdl mxhxdl
h7 ;d;[figpg igpghkfj ;d;[figpg ;d;[figpg ;d;[figpg
ydi hkfjkkl; kkl;xcvl; hkfjkkl; hkfjkkl; hkfjkkl;
ouf xcvl;xvc xvcklxcv xcvl;xvc xcvl;xvc xcvl;xvc
dui- klxcvkl klkl;ckl; klxcvkl klxcvkl klxcv[p
etryhop kl;ckl;kl kl;kl;xcv kl;ckl;kl kl;ckl;kl hjkasd
edrthyr ;kl;xcvk ki0i[xd[o ;kl;xcvk ;kl;xcvk ooas9
ijhkl;;x i0i[xd[o odlocoo[ i0i[xd[o i0i[xd[o i0-0
mxhxdl odlocoo[ phjkahd odlocoo[ odpaias
;d;[figpg phjkasd hxcsygy phjkasd i0icppa
hkfjkkl; yutuiw dyggyus jkhsdg jgruye

## A Bent Mystery

bzx bzx bzx bzx bzx bzx bvlbxllh bvlbxl
bvlb bvlb bvlb bvlb bvlb bvlb uighkb uighkb
xllh xllh xllh xllh xllh xllhkll bz
juig juig juig juig juig juigjhg bvlb
hkb hkb hkb hkb hkb hkbyre xllh
oigh oigh oigh oigh oigh oighofp juig
uggi uggi\uggi uggi uggi uggidse hkb

# 8

## H Publishing

Publisher: H Publishing
         605 Clinton Street,
         Denver, Colorado 80247.

First Printing: 2016
Kindle: 2018

___  Library of Congress Cataloging in Publication Data
     Bathhouse Bloodbath!: A Bent Mystery: a novel/ Ken
Lansdowne
         p.  cm.
     ISBN: 978-0-9740853-8-8
     1. Title

Printed in USA                          H Publishing

## BOOKS BY THE AUTHOR

### Jacob Marley
A Gay Victorian Christmas Novella

## THE BENT MYSTERY SERIES:

Secrets Don't Belong In Closets
A Murderous Ball Of Fluff
The Fairy Dust Killer
Home Sweet Homo
Dance:Ten  Murder:Maybe?
A Mystery, Wrapped In A Mystery,
 Surrounded By A Mystery
The Art of Death
Bathhouse Bloodbath!

## I

When Whiney McDrinky—Not his real name, of course. It is an anonymous program after all —began sharing the same complaints as his share from the week before Len got up from his seat in the back row to wander over to the hospitality table.

That's where his sponsor, Jerry G—no last names. Anonymous, remember—was busily replenishing the cookie tray. For some reason gay AA often reminded Len of small-town Elk and Moose camaraderie clubs. Admittedly, not quite as much fun without the boozy war stories, but that was part of the price for being sober in the program. The only thing missing at these AA meetings was a secret handshake and the silly hats.

Jerry attending to the cookies was an example of the "being of service" part of AA. That is one of the tenets of the program. Len poured himself a Styrofoam cup of hot water and began to dunk a tea bag in it while perusing a couple of the brochures fanned out on the table for the members. *How AA Works* and *The Steps Are There To Help* were the titles that caught his eye.

It turned out there were some conditions to being sober they don't advertise in the brochures. A whole set of what they like to call *suggestions* that need to be taken up so you might achieve what the program promises. And, if Len had to be truthful with himself, it was that promise of a new life he was seeking in the AA rooms. He wanted to regain his ability to be in charge of his own life. His days as a drunken flibbity-gibbitt had grown as thin as the bald spot at the back of his head. Len had come to prefer not having his days controlled by alcohol or any of the rest of the mind altering stuff available on the streets of New York.

Because—to be as honest as the program told him he should be—standing around a church social hall on Christopher Street at a Monday night gay AA meeting was not Len's idea of a terrific way to spend his day off from the show he was currently playing in. But Jerry G., his sponsor—one more thing the program *suggests*. You should get a watcher. They call him a sponsor. It's less coercive sounding that way. He's a someone you're encouraged to report to at the end of each day. Mostly the calls consist of saying "I didn't drink today", but other times you end up in conversations that go deeper into your life. Len had figured out Jerry was probing for his reasons for drinking beyond just being really really thirsty.

The night before, quicker that Len could get off the line, Jerry had asked him to be at this meeting tonight. So, accommodating soul that he was, Len had schlepped over to the subway and came down to the Village that evening from the upper East Side where he lived. He did wonder what it was that Jerry wanted with him?

The meeting now over the assembled group stood to hold hands while reciting the Serenity Prayer, then finished with "Keep coming back. It works if you work it." said in unison.

I know. It does sound kinda cult like, doesn't it? Len had decided if AA was indeed a cult it was a pretty benign one. Sort of a Mac-cult.

The thirty or so men started gathering their belongings, stacking folding chairs, cleaning the tables, picking up ashtrays, and exiting the church. He and Jerry finished their chores by rinsing out the coffee urn, then locking it away for another week. They then left the church to walk across Sheridan Square and go to the *Bagel &* cafe for coffee and talk.

As they walked into the building Len was again amazed that what was now a well-lit restaurant was once upon a time known as The Stonewall Inn. It was the site of one of the most important events in modern gay history. There was no vestige of the gay bar left anymore, only white and chrome refrigerated iron-lung looking cabinets that held slices of plastic looking desserts set on white lace paper doilies. There was no plaque commemorating the history of the building. No indication that in this place eighteen years before was where the beginning of the gay movement started on a sultry summer night in 1969.

Jerry and Len got a fresh bagel each. Onion for him, cinnamon raisin for Len—Len, you have to know, is one of those back in the hills Missabama Southern *goyim* transplanted to New York, so we'll be nice here and give him a little slack on his bagel choice—plus coffee for both. While they made their way to an empty table they greeted other program members at other table's—men they knew from meetings—then sat together to have their confab. The Bagel was a popular place for the AA crowd because the owners didn't mind that the newly sober queens would nurse a single cup of coffee for hours as they congregated and talked the nights away at their tables.

Jerry got right to his point. "So how are you doing?" It was the duty of a sponsor to monitor the first days of a person's sobriety and then guide them through the rest of the process. Jerry was damn good at his job.

"I'm sober today, so that's an accomplishment."

"What's it been now. Several months, right?"

"Four months two weeks and three days. Do you want the hours and minutes too?"

Jerry smiled. Newbies were always this precise

about their days in the beginning. "Not necessary. I just hadn't heard from you in a few days and wanted to make sure you were all right. You know you're supposed to call me every day, don't you?"

"We spoke last night," Len said defensively. He added, "I'm surprised you still want to hear from me all the time."

"Well, I do. It's important we keep in touch."

"Really? I'd think you'd be bored with me by now. I am doing okay you know? My show keeps me busy, and I haven't wanted to drink or drug." After his slip a few months earlier Len felt confident he had the basics down now. Don't drink and go to meetings. He said as much to Jerry, then added, "I've been making at least a meeting a day. Sometimes two or three when I feel I need them."

Jerry leaned forward, putting his arms on the table. "That's what I like to hear from my sponsees. But that only covers the first step, Len. Admitting you are powerless. But there's more to it than just that. You know there are twelve steps to the process in total."

Len nodded. He'd seen the white, black, and red vinyl coated listing of the steps at every meeting he'd attended.

Jerry went on. "I think it might be time for you to start looking at steps two through twelve. Especially four and nine."

"What are those?"

"Taking a personal inventory and making amends. Both very important to your sobriety..."

Jerry and Len had continued to talk for an hour or more, covering a wide range of topics between them. Everything from the backstage gossip at Len's show to digging out events put into boxes and left unexamined for many years in the back of Len's brain. Jerry was excellent at finding the triggers that could set Len off. But tempered it by also giving him ways to cope and work his way past them rather than go down the rabbit hole again. Len promised to call his sponsor each evening and to read the steps for himself.

They parted soon after.

The next day Len went downstairs to his friend JB's apartment for their usual morning gossip and coffee klatch. Jeremy Bent—JB to his friends—was that morning in one of his more turbid moods. He had put out the Danish and a so-so blend of Colombian, but hadn't been particularly forthcoming with the schmoozing part of the morning.

"What's wrong with you today?"

"I don't know. I just feel blaagh..." JB put a guttural velar on the final gh. Then, to put icing on the sound, followed it with a sigh.

Len, sitting across the table from him, held up two of his fingers in the classic sign of the cross. The universal symbol used to keep vampires or illness at bay. "You're not coming down with anything, are you?"

Len, as a working actor currently employed on the Broadway stage knew that he needed to keep himself cold free as a job requirement. "I have to work tonight, you know? Pneumonia isn't an option for me." He dropped his religious stance. "Although, to be honest, I'm not all that sure it really matters so much anymore. The rumors at work say we'll be posting notice any day now."

JB looked up from contemplating his own dilemma. "So you were right. With Lee gone from the show you said you wouldn't stay open for long."

The show's star, Lee Arden, had left to attend to a personal matter. At least that's what the publicity department put out to the press. The real reason was more along the lines that her son was dying from AIDS, and she felt it was her job to gently help her child through his final passage. Her understudy had replaced her.

"We can't keep going, JB. We've been bleeding money for a week now. Without a star in the lead the ticket sales have dropped precipitously. Well, you know how expensive the show is. Oh, its gonna close all right. And in the next few weeks."

"That may not be the only reason. I stopped in to watch a scene at your last matinee. I think I actually heard one whole line that I'd written. You've all gotten a bit fast and loose with the script, you know?" JB had been hired to be the show's "doctor"—rewriting and updating the script back when it was still in rehearsals.****

Len hurumped. "Only to wring a few laughs out of your deathless prose. Or should I say deadly?" He slunk down in his chair. "So, I will soon be at liberty once again. Ah, such is life upon the wicked stage"— this was said as dramatically as possible, complete with a sans souci gesture of back of hand to forehead. Len could get very grand on occasion—"Is it too much to ask to be steadily employed in one's chosen profession? Talk about a person deserving to have the blaaghs," he groused.

"Not fair. You can't have them while I have them. Anyway, the blaaghs I have aren't the contagious kind of blaaghs. Mine are more of a greenish malodorous gritty yucky variety of the blaaghs. I just feel sort of oocky, you know?"

"And those are the medical terms, are they?" Len asked.

"I don't know, Len, it's as if something should be happening and it isn't. I feel like I'm in some waiting room where I'm to be assigned my next life task." JB sighed again. "And considering the circumstances I probably won't do much better than air conditioner repairman. It's that kind of blaaghs."

"You know, for a simi-renowned writer you have a completely unique way with the American idiom. It is truly a marvel to behold."

JB, or Jeremy Bent, was the creator of a series of murder mystery novels that sold well enough to keep the proverbial wolf from his New York City apartment door. As if any wolf other than a Wall Street type would be found in all of New York to begin with.

****For this part of the story see *Dance:Ten, Murder: Maybe?* Number 5 in the Bent Mystery series.

JB answered Len. "I use words that are on point as to the feeling I am currently experiencing."—JB could get haughty himself at times—"I couldn't be any clearer."

"So, if I go to my trusty Webster's and looked in the B's I would find the word *blaagh?*"

"With my picture next to it," JB answered, not giving up.

"Not to mention oocky? What the hell kind of word is that?"

The two men were sitting at JB's kitchen table sipping coffee on a morning in late summer. Outside Manhattan was just beginning to feel the effects of the rapidly approaching autumn. It was 1987 and there was already enough cold on a morning to require a jacket against a chill that would completely dissipate only a few hours later. Which would then leave you stuck lugging the now unnecessary garment over your shoulder for the rest of the day. All while being shoved, yelled at, pushed aside, banged into, and flipped off in several different languages. Ahh, we do so love our city don't we fair citizens?

"Well, JB, I am fully aware of the origins of my blaaghs. I'm losing my friggin' job. But yours? From whence do it spring, huh?" Len held up a finger. "Wait, I think I may have it. You're just bored aren't you?"

"Len, it's nothing so simple as plain old boredom." He scratched at the back of his head. "It's more like an unease. That's it. I'm feeling restive. Tired. Inured. On edge. Would you like I should continue?"

Len held up a hand. "Not necessary. And when are you going to learn to take a joke? At the very least when I hang around with you I never need a thesaurus."

"A synonym finder. A..."

"Now cut that out." Len said, doing a more than credible Jack Benny impression.

JB laughed. Len went on.

"Although, I do think I know what's bugging you. There's some sort of mental thing going on with you, isn't there?"

"And that's what you think it is Madam Freud?"

This kind of bickering was a staple between the two men. A signpost to the kind of friends JB and Len were with each other. Despite—or because of—a past where they had been involved as lovers these two gay men still managed to be the best of friends. In fact, Len, well known among the New York theater crowd, and JB, an equally well known writer among his own crowd, were close enough to think of each other as brothers. Or better yet, because of their being gay—and the homosexual penchant for using feminine pronouns wherever possible—they were great big sisters. Family. You know?

Len, seeing his glib psychoanalysis wasn't getting him anywhere, decided to try a different tact. "When was the last time you went anywhere, JB? You really do need to get out more. You stay cooped up in this apartment for days on end, completely cut off from the world. You don't go out. When's the last time you had a date?"

"Len, I really don't think of myself as being cut off from the world. I prefer to think I'm working diligently to create a world that's worthy of my living in it. I'm engineering a world that addresses my needs entirely, thereby eliminating all that other extraneous folderol. Anyway, not all of us can be the social butterfly you are. Human interaction can be difficult for some of us."

"Well, not calling it a human interaction might go a long way toward making it less difficult." Len reached across the table and tapped JB's hand. "I've got an idea..."

"And you want to toss it around and see if we get tuna salad."

"More like chicken with a side of little or no dressing."

"What the hell are you talking about?"

Len answered, paraphrasing an old vaudeville joke, "Do the name Dimity London ring a familiar note?"

JB took a moment to ponder the question. "Dimity London? She's a singer, right? There was an article about her in the *Village Voice* last week."

"That's the one. She's appearing at Aesop's Atrium

over on the West Side..."

Aesop's Atrium was a relatively well known gay bathhouse located in the basement of the Astonia Hotel and Apartment building. The hotel itself had stood on the corner of 74th and Broadway since the late 1890's when it was initially erected by one of the last of the Gilded Age robber barons, a cohort of Diamond Jim Brady and Boss Tweed. The hotel's penthouse also became notorious as the location, during the Roaring Twenties, of the rather messy murder of a George White chorus girl. The deed was done by the rich son of the building's original architect. He was a degenerate wastrel keeping the chorus girl as his mistress—or as a sex slave according to the *Police Gazette* articles of the time. The chorine was murdered by her paramour after being discovered swinging from a crystal chandelier and drinking bootleg booze from a loving cup won by her other lover, a local jockey out at the Aqueduct Raceway. Tre scandalous

The bathhouse had opened in the building and became popular during the sexual revolution of the 1970's. Open to all sorts of carrying on's it had fallen on hard times after the AIDS crisis had struck the city in the early 80's.

"...you and I should go see this Dimity woman tonight," Len concluded.

"She's appearing at the tubs?" JB said doubtfully. "Didn't Bette Midler already do that? Sure she did. At the Continental Baths. Years and years ago."

"Indeed. It is a sort of Midler re dux, isn't it? Perhaps it's homagé to the true diva Bette has managed to make of herself in the last few years. This London woman is making a return to another person's roots so to speak. What worked for the goose?"

Theater, and the cabaret scene for that matter, in New York has always been able to adapt to the changing times that rush around it. Revues were popular in the 20's so every theater between 42nd and 53rd Street was running a Ziegfeld or Earl Carroll extravaganza. The people wanted dramas? The 50's had Tennessee Williams, William Inge, and Arthur Miller. Likewise, the

60's were stuffed with musicals from talents the likes of Steven Sondheim and Jerry Herman.

Now, in the 80's, with the high cost of mounting any production there has been a turn to the cheaper Off and Off-Off Broadway theaters. *Forbidden Broadway*, a popular spoof of the current Broadway season, is running in a little ninety seat nightclub on West 72nd Street. An abandoned church in the Village has been taken over and is playing *Steve and Sandy's Wedding*, an interactive evening where the paying audience are treated as the guests at the catered Waspish affair. And, it now appeared that up and coming starlets were once more singing in homosexual bathhouses.

And getting rave reviews while doing so Len pointed out. Those superlative reviews had served to make Dimity London the one to be seen by the cognoscenti who mattered. Celebrities like Jackie O and Liza M had been seen sitting next to men wrapped in nothing more than thin towels. It had to be a sight to see.

"...So, JB," Len was saying. "You'll come to the theater tonight after curtain and we'll go to the tub's together. We can see the midnight show. Should be fun, don't ja think?" Len twirled his hand in the trademark Bette Davis hand gesture.

"Wow," JB shook his head. "I swear, Len, there isn't any part of the gay stereotype you don't fit is there?"

<big><big><big>II</big></big></big>

he leather heels of JB and Len's shoes clicked on thousands upon thousands of white hexagon penny sized tiles that had been laid as the original flooring of the Astonia Hotel. A key and wheat decorative pattern in black tile ran along the edges under rococo gilded wood half tables with verdigris framed mirrors hung above them. These were interspersed with Greek topped plaster columns running up to a coved and skyscaped painted ceiling with gold leafed stars glinting from the recessed lights.

However, it was evident that the columns were looking a bit dinged and chipped. The ceiling stars were starting to fade. The mirrors had turned frosty. Regardless, the hallway still held on to remnants of the elegance the builders put into the place in its heyday. But now the smell of pine disinfectant and an underlayer of what JB's nose told him was a cooked vegetable emanated down from the upstairs apartments and permeated the air. The old girl was definitely seeing her last days. She was in need of a major makeover.

A twisted iron balustrade lined a worn marble stairway that circled down to the building's basement floor. This was where the entrance to the Atrium bathhouse was located. A box office style barred window had a T-shirt clad young man standing behind it. He took JB's and Len's $15.00 cover fee and gave them two drink tickets in return. Then he pressed a buzzer that echoed in the cavern of the lower hallway. A metal clad door beside the window clicked open for them to enter.

Inside the decor would be called by *Architectural Digest* "a mid-Regency Fairyland". Gleaming white rectangular subway tiles entirely covered the walls from ceiling to floor, with a double trim line in school bus yellow running waist high around the perimeter.

Four huge rectangular columns, two on each end of the open main room, were also coated in the slick white tiles. The columns held up a second floor balcony that circled the space with a staircase at each end for access. Up there a gilded railing with decorative Edwardian cast iron lampposts marched around the balcony edge. Fake flower and ivy swags were strung between the lampposts.

The lower central area had more of the same subway tiles covering five terraced steps, which made for a theater in the round with the stage situated at the bottom of the pit. Gold tasseled throw pillows were slung about the steps, provided for the audience to sit on or lean against. All very Roman baths in feel the only things missing were toga clad servant boys to peel and feed the patrons bunches of grapes.

Overhead, tiny lights were strung and mixed in with leafy artificial branches, giving the ceiling the impression of a Van Gogh night sky and forest canopy overhead. Which was enough to justify the atrium moniker of what on close inspection was a completely windowless basement.

A partially glass enclosed juice and liquor bar was located straight to the left of the entrance door. A couple of well-muscled servers stood at the bar wearing skimpy towels around their waists instead of the aforementioned togas. Several hallways cut into the perimeter of the ground floor. These led off to the steam room, a heated pool, the *Jacuzzi*, a weight room, and various other specialty rooms suited to the bathhouse and its particular clientele—meaning you would probably find a dungeon, a sling room, and other more kink specific areas back among the dimly lit halls.

The locker area was directly across the center pit right next to the frosted glass steam room door and the open showers. The whole place had an antiseptically humid feeling and smelled, well—moist. The wet was underlined with the odor of old amyl nitrite capsules mixed with a tinge of stale sweat. Not Chanel N° 5, but also not so unpleasant to the particular clientele mentioned earlier.

It being a weekday night the show area wasn't all that crowded. The late show, according to a poster set on an easel by the bar, would begin in fifteen minutes. There were one or two clusters of what had to be that night's audience seated on the steps. Dressed in civilian clothes they included several women among their number. The women had gathered tightly on the side closest to the door. Whether this was for social reasons, or was an overt example of the human predilection for crowding together for comfort wasn't really clear. They were, however, all clutching their pillows as pouffy shields in front of themselves, while tittering and pointing to the towel clad men, as if they were part of a road company of Gilbert and Sullivan players doing *Three Little Maids* from *The Mikado*.

Twelve or so nearly naked men were gathered in their own groups on the other side of the show pit. They were also tittering and pointing. Each group was taking great pleasure in making judgments about the other. Which group would turn out to be the freak du jour would largely depend on what your particular proclivities were, the same way as how long a minute can be depends on which side of the bathroom door you're standing on.

JB and Len took their seats in neutral territory. They were comfortable there until a young man in a gold lamé jacket tapped Len on the shoulder and said, "I'm sorry, gentlemen, but down this way is where Ms. London will be making her entrance. Could I ask you to move over a couple of feet?" Then his eyes got that wide-eyed look of recognition, and he went on. "Hey, you're Len Matthews, aren't you? Dimity will be thrilled that you've come to see her show. I know she'll want to introduce you. Will that be all right?"

"Of course," Len said, always willing to lean over backward for a bit of applause. Then, in a fit of unaccustomed charity, he added, "You might want to mention that the famous writer Jeremy Bent is here too." Len held his hand in JB's direction with what could be recognized as one of Len's more obnoxious smirks. JB knew he was figuring that should any of the New York tabloids catch them there in the bath's JB's name would also be implicated in any stories they printed.

The young man was looking down at the stage, checking on the rest of the musicians just getting set up. The band consisted of a drummer and a bass player along with two women and a man, a threesome of backup singers. The boy singer got JB's attention right away. Pretty men would always do that for him.

The young man standing above JB and Len then had to be the piano player, and the leader of the group. His head pulled back to face Len. "Who did you say?" He looked over at JB. "Jeremy Bent, you said?" He smiled. "Well, sure, the mystery writer guy, right? She sure will." He grinned again at them. The smile managed to give a quick charm to his rather ordinary looks. Heavy Buddy Holly type glasses were really the only interesting thing about his face. He then quickly turned and bounced down the steps to take his place at the piano and start tuning up his group of musicians.

"A nice enough young man, I would say. If not a bit on the Liberace side in that jacket."

"No, not really. You know without the candelabra on the piano he can only manage to be a pale Elvis. He did seem nice enough though. Gay do you think?"

"Well, I don't think he would be out of place in the

first row of a Cher concert."

"And need I direct your attention to that boy singer down there? Take a good look at that succulent piece of man flesh, will you." A lascivious little grin shuttered JB's lips.

Len took an appraising look. The boy JB was pointing out was tall and slender with a naturally muscled body under a glittery shirt open to the navel. His blond hair was cut in what was called a mullet, long in back, and with enough product in the front to cause an oil slick on the Gulf of Mexico. A square jaw, high cheekbones, and hooded sensual eyes combined to make him very handsome indeed. "Yes, JB, he is quite nice, but I'm surprised at you. That you noticed him at all. I mean didn't you, just a day ago, say you had given up sex for good?"

"Just because I've been neutered doesn't mean I can't go to the end of my chain barking at the passing cars."

The band leader in the lamé jacket struck the piano keys to play a bright arpeggio. The bass player started to pluck a low beat, the drummer kept time. Then, underlying the music, catching the melody, the voice of Dimity London came from somewhere behind JB and Len. She was singing *"Gee, But It's Good To Be Here,"* the opening number from a 1950's Ethel Merman musical called *Happy Hunting.*

The singer finally appeared at the top of the steps holding a cordless mic in her hand. She was wearing a floaty blue beaded and chiffon multi-layered cocktail creation that went a long way toward covering what was kindly called her corpulent shape. The girl was definitely on the heavy side. At only twenty she had just the month before been the cover model for *Big Beautiful Girl* magazine, a newish publication aimed at something other than the anorexic thin model types usually featured on fashion covers. A mass of almost kinky, bleached white blond hair was piled on top of her head, held there with a sparkle of rhinestones that reflected like a disco ball in the spotlight shining on her. Expertly applied makeup was making her to prominent nose a kinder shape.

However, even with the application of several sets of artificial eyelashes and a pouty red painted mouth Dimity still only managed striking rather than beautiful. It was her voice not her looks that was her selling point. Her voice was a mid-alto with a range that could soar all the way up to an airy soprano. This gave her the ability to have both a belt and a head voice and a very wide singing range of several octaves. Her voice was quite able to wring every note she sang of every bit of its subtly and nuance. She could make you applaud a raucous Merman show-stopper one moment and then turn around to sigh with a Barbara Cook softly sung heartwrencher the next. She was the latest show-biz wiz, a bawdy, funny, whirlwind of a rising new talent who at this stage of her career was in the process of making herself famous. The kind that at dinner parties ten years further on you could say you knew she was a star even then.

She continued singing the snappy opening song as she made her way down the steps to dance around the piano. She ended with a grand flourish in the curve of the instrument, raising her arm in a gesture right out of the Judy Garland "Man That Got Away" song book.

JB leaned over and said to Len as he clapped for her entrance, "She certainly knows what her audience wants, doesn't she? But Garland must be plotzing in her grave right about now."

Then, as if to attribute JB with some psychic power, Dimity launched into *The Trolley Song*, from *Meet Me In St. Louis*, a Garland standard. As she sang it she even managed to give her voice a hint of that quavering tone that Judy herself was so famous for. Another of Dimity's claims to her rapturous reviews was her uncanny ability to channel other singer's styles. She was already well known for her Ella Fitzgerald like scat singing, also for a Kate Smith clarion like belt. Now it appeared she'd added Garland's vulnerable longing to her repertoire of cloned styles. Would "Weird Al" Yankovic be next?

For the next forty-five minutes the appreciative audience, including Len, were buoyantly and riotously entertained by Dimity London's talents. She sang the old standards and even did a standup routine of jokes, working them as homagé to another lady comic, channeling a really credible Todie Fields, the 1960's comedienne. Dimity took her audience happily to gales of laughter and applause. She entertained them the same way Cohan and Jolson and Sophie Tucker did back in their day, by dint of her own singular talent.

As she went into a final reprieve of the Merman opener for her finish the audience was clamoring for more. She bowed and thanked and decided to encore with *Don't Rain On My Parade* from *Funny Girl*. A plucky choice. The song was a challenge for any singer to live up to after Streisand had finished with it. But Dimity managed to almost match Barbra with her own power and timber. Her effort brought the audience to its collective feet again. Except for JB who remained seated.

As Len sat back down, he said, "It was a wonderful show don't you think, JB?"

"Yeah. It was cute. It was fun. It was like spending time with a rainbow."

"Wow. And they call me critical. I take it you weren't all that amused by her performance?"

"It was okay, but..."

"There's always one of those buts with you, isn't there?"

"But. Come on, Len, she's already canned and on the shelf at half price. She's way to slick already. And she's only just begun, to quote Karen Carpenter. What I really object to is there's absolutely no sincerity anywhere near that entire act. It's all so calculated. She's just another baby diva. Cher should be watching her back."

"Don't hold it in, JB."

"Well, you stood for her. I couldn't stand her. Its all a matter of opinion. Now, if you really want my opinion...that boy singer..." JB moved his hand up and down as he again pointed him out. "With him I would go so far as to use the phrase hummana, hummana, hummana."

"I would have to agree with you. But I'm surprised. He's not your usual type at all."

"Beauty is as beauty is, Len. I will always rise for a truly beautiful man when I see one."

And Dimity's male back-up singer was exactly that in JB's opinion. Blessed by whichever of the Gods that control physical allure, he was given his looks in a triple dose. There are certain people that are so beautiful the whole world just hands itself over to them. Hedy Lamarr, Grace Kelly, Clark Gable—truly stunning people that will always cause the human saliva gland to work overtime. "What did Dimity say his name was?"

"She didn't. She just said he was one of the Sluttones. I think I begin to see that diva thing you were saying about her. Wouldn't even introduce her back-up singers by name? Can't you just hear her? It's *my* spotlight. You stay out of it." He shrugged and added, "Actually being a diva isn't such a big deal to me. God knows I've had to work with my fair share of them. I've even been one myself on occasion. Always have. In second grade I got in trouble with my teacher because I insisted that Miss Muffett wouldn't be afraid of no damn spider. She'd just stomp down on the little bugger. I really don't mind most diva behavior as long as there's sufficient talent to back it up."

"And you think this London woman has that kind of talent?"

"I think she's well on her way..."

As they were talking they had stood and were moving over to the bar area. The rest of the audience had also risen and were going their own ways—the ladies and their escorts out to the wilds of Manhattan. The left behind towel clad men heading for the bathhouse halls to troll for tricks.

As they entered the bar Len scoped it out. The usual surveillance to see if there might be anyone interesting lingering about. He took a few more steps in and stopped cold. There was a look on his face that hovered near surprise but without the usual yelp that goes along with the emotion.

"Uh, JB, you order the drinks, okay. I'll wait over there..."

and he headed for one of the booths at the far side of the glass enclosed bar area.

JB, not thinking at all about the oddity of Len's behavior, said, "Your usual?" and went up to the bar to make his order.

A few minutes later JB set down a glass of cranberry juice with a slice of lime in front of Len and slid into the booth so he faced him. By then Len's escape to the booth had registered and he was wondering what was up. He had to ask. "So, what was that about?"

"Nothing to bother yourself over. It's just that I know that bartender over there and I would rather not run into him."

JB turned and looked at him. He was around the same age as them. Handsome in the way barkeeps and ex-actors often are. "Someone from your murky past is it?"

"What part of I don't want to see him did you not get? Don't look at him, JB. It'll just draw his attention." Len picked up his drink and took a swallow while sliding down in the booth and turning so he faced away from the bar.

"Fine. But what the hell did he do to you? Or what did you do to him?"

"It was a long time ago. Before I knew you. His name is Brian something. He wasn't a bartender when I knew him. He was another actor. I beat him out for a major part. He hasn't liked me ever since. I haven't seen him in ages and I'd rather not stir anything up, if you don't mind."

"Fine by me. But he knows you're here, Len. Dimity announced your name during her act. Remember?"

"Shit. Well, maybe he won't care."

"He comped you your drink, Len. He told me to tell you he'd like to talk. I was supposed to pass on the message."

"Double shit." He looked at his watch. "Its close to one AM, JB. Shouldn't we try for a cab home or would you rather catch a steam while we're here?"

"A steam, huh? Is that what you're calling it now? Admit it, Len, you've been horn dogging this whole night.

That's the main reason you suggested coming here in the first place, right? But I'm not so sure a steam is the only thing you're likely to catch around here."

"That's why there's a bowl of condoms over by the window. And yes, I do happen to be horny, damn it. It's been over a month since I last got laid. I just think its time to put the sex back in homosexual."

"Good God, what are you going for? Some sort of a sexual camel? Without the humps, of course."

"Do you want to stay or not?"

"I wouldn't mind staying. But what about him?" JB jerked his thumb toward the bartender.

"I'll just have to deal with him later." Len picked up his drink and slid out of the booth. "We need to sign in. Are you coming?"

"Is that coming spelled with an O or a U? Both are a possibility around here, you know?"

"That's what I'm counting on."

# III

They carried their drinks over to the window to begin the signing in process. First, they handed over their wallets and valuables to the clerk, who slipped them into individual manila envelopes and stored them in a large standing lock box. Then they signed their registration cards while also putting their names on a waiting list for a room when one might open up later. Len signed himself in as Ambrose Hamilton. They waited for the clerk to hand over their locker keys—which were attached to an elastic wrist band—along with a crispy napped slightly larger than a tea sized white towel.

It was a routine played out many times by many gay men over the years. That is until these places were shut down by city ordinance when AIDS first struck New York back in 1981. Now there were only two gay bathhouses still open in the entire city and they were so harshly regulated that attendance had become spotty at best. Hence having a variety act for a cabaret night was a way for the place to generate some revenue. It certainly wouldn't have been needed back in the days of the sexual revolution. Back when there were men who spent entire weekends at the baths, even bringing in picnic baskets of foodstuffs for Sunday brunch.

The clerk said, "We're running a bootleg of *My Beautiful Launderette* at two, if you're interested...Mr. Hamilton, is it?" He raised an eyebrow. He knew who Len was, but also knew that in case of a raid using a fake name made sure the real one wouldn't appear on any local police blotters. JB had signed in as Portnoy J. Roth. The clerk pushed out the keys and towels to them.

"And what time does the orgy start, my good man?" Len asked.

"It's run continuously since eighty-three..."

"Like a Times Square grind house movie."

"...so jump in whenever you please."

While Len was having his tête-à-tête with the bath house clerk, JB, who was standing behind him, had tuned into another conversation going on over at the end of the bar. Eavesdropping, like lying, was to JB just one more item useful to his writing arsenal. Listening in wasn't something he would indulge in on a regular basis, but it was certainly handy when it served his purpose. A snatch of overheard badinage could be the perfect way to get him out of a spot in a recalcitrant plot he might have been working on. A witty exchange between two people at the next table had saved him a few times, and the saying about old and new jokes applied equally to conversations—if you haven't heard it before then it's original.

The conversation JB had tipped to this time was between Dimity London—now out of her sparkly costume and wrapped in a flowered chenille robe—and another man.

He was medium tall, middle aged, gray at the temples, not altogether unattractive, more well groomed than handsome, with a thin line for a mouth that he attempted to cover with one of those stupid Tom Selleck type mustaches. It looked like a small bat was hanging off his nostrils. He had hard flinty eyes, and an expanding mid-life girth. He reminded JB of the Roman

God Bacchus. Friendly but boozy, soft but daunting.

It can't be easy for someone dressed in nothing more than a towel to really intimidate another person, but this guy was trying very hard to cower Ms. London. And it was obvious from her own posture that he was invading her personal space with his towering over her and glowering down.

Taking only one tiny step closer JB could clearly hear the threat in the man's tone as he spoke to her starness. Then JB saw him grab her arm and pull her in close. She gave a tiny yelp of protest, making it clear the two of them weren't playing around.

The man said to her in as menacing a voice as ever JB had heard, "I'm telling you this, and you know I mean every word, get that ample ass of yours in line, Missy. That is if you want to play that Radio City contract I got you. Keep up this other shit and you'll be kicked to the curb in a New Jersey minute. You want a career? Then you'll do as I say. Do it my way or it's a great big no way, sweetheart. Do you get it?"

Len tapped JB on the shoulder and spoke softly in his ear, "You wouldn't be thinking of interfering there would you? My advice is to stay out of it, JB. He could be dangerous."

Len was playing at being the good angel perched on JB's shoulder. But the more sinful and manipulative angel on the other side stood right up and answered back in a voice remarkably like JB's. "But he's threatening her, Len. And it isn't as if he's got any concealed weapons. Where would he hide anything in only a towel?"

"To be honest I think its kind of like Santa Claus. You don't have to see it, you just have to believe it exists."

JB had more than enough run-ins with bullies like this guy going all the way back to grammar school. He'd had forced upon him more than his share of taunts and beatings, wedgies and swirlies from one overweight pimply faced ogre of a kid who'd tipped to the fact JB was a big sissy. It made for a truly miserable time from the fourth grade on.

That went on until JB had finally stood up to his tormentor. He discovered that one hard kick to the crotch and the boy never bothered him again. Now, even after all these supposed years of more civilized behavior, JB was seeing someone else using the same sort of tactics on this poor woman. That meant she was in peril, and it was his duty as another put-upon minority to protect her if he could, wasn't it?

Besides, JB was well aware that there were enough witnesses around to keep the man from doing any real harm to him. A threat of legal action and assault charges was usually enough to stop most threatened attacks from actually happening.

JB stepped up to the couple. "Are you all right, Ms. London? Can I be of some help?"

She turned to face him, clutching at the opening of her robe. The anger that had been coloring her face was quickly substituted with something meaning to be much friendlier. She nervously smiled. "No, I'm fine, but aren't you sweet for offering. This gentleman and I were just discussing some personal business. He sometimes loses all control of his senses." She twisted back to face him. Her teeth clenched tightly she said, "You should know, when I want it enough, I will always get my way, Matty. In fact, I plan on being in the *Guinness Book Of World Records* for exactly that accomplishment."

The man spoke from the side of his mouth, "What 'world's biggest bitch' was already taken?"

Dimity looked down her substantial nose at him. "My friend, you will regret saying that." On that note Dimity turned on a mule covered heel and stomped off.

The two men, JB and Matty, were left standing together looking down at their toes, until JB broke the embarrassed impasse and looked the man straight in the face. JB needed to find a civilized way out of the mess his apparently needless interfering in their argument had ended up being.

At a loss for words, what JB really wanted to do was make sure Matty got what he had meant to say to begin with. That was—Okay, you get away with it this time, bunko, but act like that to a defenseless woman again and, to paraphrase *The Iliad,* there is no weapon, no army that can protect you from the sheer hell that is Jeremy Bent's rage. JB would have assured him he would make it his life's ambition to find a sharp instrument and plunge it deep into Matty's spleen, thereby making sure he became permanently among the dearly departed. Gone to a better place—or to some unknowable dark abyss that awaits us all. Whichever came first.

Instead JB just shrugged and grinned.

Matty squared his bare shoulders, then cinched tighter the towel draped around his hips. With a toss of his head, he said, "What a bitch, huh? Sometimes I just want to kill her..." He held out a hand. "I'm Matty Silverman. I have the horror of being that hags fag. And her manager."

JB smiled. "I've heard that fairy consort is the proper title these days"

Matty chuckled and wiped at the perspiration on his forehead. "Well..." He took a look at the expensive watch that hung off his arm like a Cartier bracelet. The man was wearing not only the watch, but a flashy gold ring, a diamond ear stud, and a silver nipple barbell on his chest. It was a choice if a patron wanted his belongings kept behind the desk. Which reminded JB he had been checking in. "Well. I was..." He gestured toward the check-in window

Matty caught the drift, and said, "...if you'll excuse me, I have an appointment with a man upstairs. Of course, first I'm gonna have to get him boiled." He tsked. "Sex used to be so much more fun before..." He smiled, which showed a row of capped teeth like little white tombstones running along inside his lips. He turned, and headed for the stairs. The cubicles were to be found upstairs. He quickly disappeared into the warren of hallways that held them.

The Atrium's second floor was made up of hallway after hallway of unpainted plywood doors with hardware store numbers screwed on to them—some doors were open, some shut. Behind them you would find a slit of a space with a built-in wooden palette and a small shelf next to it. Along the wall were a couple of wire hooks for your clothes in a room so tiny it would give a mouse a hunchback. A thin cot type mattress covered with a twin sheet and a case less travel pillow finished off the scant accommodations. The purpose of these rooms certainly wasn't comfort. What they did offer was privacy. The rooms provided a place to take someone interesting and have sex with them without other greedy hands pawing at you in the dark of the orgy rooms.

The tubs, as the baths are called in the gay vernacular, are a hotbed of hot beds. They could better be called the *Supermarket Sweep* of gay life. A virtual marketplace of sexual opportunities. The tubs are the sort of place Gramps warned you about as a boy. But then Gramps was warning you about women and booze, and didn't say one word about men and cocaine.

Matty Silverman was soon lost among the endless corridors.

# IV

Once the show was over the bathhouse went into a more tranquil mode while waiting for the next influx of patrons to arrive at 4AM when the city's bar's closed. Until that time the star attraction of the evening program became SEX—capitalization intended—and its various acts. This would be of such a serious endeavor that a damp blanket of urgency would descend on the entire building while these going's on's were going on.

For their part, JB and Len found their assigned lockers so they could undress and store their clothes. They each took a quick shower and then dried off with the towel supplied. Neither of them would have admitted it, but this had less to do with hygiene than because a damp towel will drape on the waist better than a dry one. It would better outline the goods, so to speak. The baths were, for all intent's and purposes, a meet market after all. And this was neither JB's or Len's first time at this particular rodeo—which they both were well aware would begin in the leather room later if they were interested.

Next, the two men took a leisurely strolling tour of the building. Getting the lay of the land before the lay of the man. That accomplished they wish the other good night and each would go off to attend to anything they might have seen on their earlier reconnaissance.

As JB roamed the halls, peeking into open doors at the merchandise displayed in corners and cubicles, he realized that he hadn't been to the tubs for quite a while. Why was that? Only a year or two before he would have spent a couple of weekends a month in their steamy environment. Nowadays he tended to spend more of his time at home with a trick towel, lube, and his VCR.

The reason, he had to admit, was that the draw of the tubs for him had always been the voyeuristic component they offered. Getting off wasn't always the main goal. Watching others do it was.

JB paced the bathhouse halls and soon began to feel the insistent rhythm of the place invade his being. The pulse in the air always awakened deeply held longings in him. Longings beckoned by the thrum of the primal urge. But he couldn't decide if it all wasn't the drum beat on the constantly running music track the bath's provided or the pulse of the wanton sex happening everywhere charging the atmosphere with a heady scent of lust and appetite? Any night spent at the tubs was a success for him if he was able to slide across from two men engaged in pleasuring themselves. The thrill for him was in the observation. Seeing hot men get it on was a bit like Nirvana for JB. When the lighting was exactly right to bring out the art of sex—men's bodies entwined, muscles tensing, straining with lust—all so beautifully going on before him he would be one contented puppy. Lately though, with VCR's at record low prices and videos available in every Times Square porn shop, his desire to watch was satisfied much easier. And he didn't have to dress up or comb his hair. He had the feeling that the world was insidiously becoming more and more isolating each passing day. Or that he was a very cheap date.

# V

The gunshot loudly cracked in the still quiet that held the bathhouse in its thrall. The din of the explosion had to be louder than the person firing it must have thought it would be or certainly he would have used some sort of silencer to muffle the sound. The bang of the shot was loud enough to stop sex acts, cause closed doors to be flung open by sleepy-eyed patrons, and make those few who were watching the bootleg movie downstairs sit up to look for the source of the noise.

The staff, knowing the layout of the place, were able to locate that source in moments. Second floor, right rear hallway.

What they found was a locked door baring their entrance to the cubical. This required one of the staff to return to the front for the master key. Meanwhile, a crowd of ten or so men had gathered waiting for a peek into the room for themselves. They waited to see what had happened to cause such a kerfuffle in the quiet of the night.

Once the key arrived there was a further

hindrance, a blockage of some sort holding the door shut, preventing entrance. They had to use a two man push to force the door open even a slight foot or two, opened enough to let a head and an arm holding a flashlight to squeeze in and look around.

"There's a body...No, two bodies...." The staff person slipped back out of the narrow opening. There was a twinge of fear quivering his voice. "From what I could see we really need to get in there. Right away."

The onlookers mumbled among themselves. Passing on what little information they could to each other. You know the answer to the old question: How do you get a message out at the speed of light? Telegraph. Telephone. Tell a queen. Although, at this point, all the information these queens could send consisted of guesses and hearsay.

Another of the staff finally arrived with a screwdriver and quickly bent to diligently work at removing the hinges from the door frame.

It was at this point that JB walked up and stood next to Len, who, not surprisingly, happened to be among the small crowd of onlookers.

With the door off its hinges the inside of the room was finally there for all to see. And damned unnerving it turned out to be.

On the mattress was a dead man, naked, with a gun blast to his face effectively obliterating any chance of easily identifying him. Blood stains and brain spatter made a gruesome halo on the wall behind the man's limp inert body.

Down on the floor lay another man. This one was leaning against the wall, and he wasn't dead, only passed out. His head lolled to one side, his breathing steady. He still had his towel wrapped at his waist which you'd think would have afforded him a bit more dignity than his dead partner. That might have been the case except that his legs were splayed wide open, splitting the towel and affording full penile exposure. Also, to add a bit of mystery to the pornographic scenario, in his hand was resting a pistol.

The most obvious conclusion to be reached was that the guy on the floor had shot the man on the bed.

JB shook his head and said to no one in particular. "I don't get it. How do they live with themselves?"

Len turned to him. "Who?"

"Whoever the killer is. How do they do something like that..." He indicated the carnage in the room. "...and then live with themselves? Hell, I still feel guilt over some Hubba-Bubba gum I took from the five and dime when I was nine. How does a murderer get through a day with that kind of grief chewing on his psyche? How do they not just kill themselves from the guilt?"

"Well, I would think there's a very wide chasm in the perpetrators moral compass, wouldn't you? I'll bet killing themselves doesn't even enter their deranged little minds."

"Well, I would sure think about it."

"And how would you do it...kill yourself that is?"— Len could play straight man with the best of them. Just don't ask him to be a straight man.

JB hit the punchline. "With kindness, my friend. Very gentle kindness. But then I didn't do that." He indicated the man on the cot and shuttered. "Len, remind me again about how you were saying my life is so sheltered."

"Who is the dead guy?" Another person in the crowd was asking the obvious next question.

One of the staff, reading from a registration card he held, said, "The room is signed out to someone named Joseph Nameth. It's not the football player is it?"

There was a derisive laugh. "Is he wearing a pair of panty hose? If he ain't, it ain't him."

The man on the floor, who up to then had a shoulder against the wall holding him upright, now slid backward. The slide backward made his face visible to the onlookers crowded at the door. They took a group step back.

JB grabbed at Len's arm. "Hey, we know him. It's the piano player from the show? What was his name? You must remember?"

"I think Dimity did mention it. What was it she called him? Was it Harry? Or Henry? Anyway, I do know his last name was Lavender. I wasn't going to forget that anytime soon." He snapped a finger. "Henry Lavender. That was it. JB?"

JB was now more engaged in looking at the body of the dead man on the bed. "And him, Len. The dead guy? You know what? I think he's that man we met before. The one who said he was Dimity's manager. You remember, he was arguing with her? He said his name was what? Buddy? No, that's not it." His forehead furrowed as he was thinking. "Matty? Matty Silverman. That's it."

"How do you know that's him? You can't see his face anymore. It's been shot off. Completely and utterly."

"Look at his chest. His right nipple specifically. It's pierced with a barbell. I remember Silverman had one."

"Well, he isn't the only gay man to have a nipple pierced here tonight. Or any other bodily protuberance for that matter. I hear a Prince Albert piercing is becoming increasingly popular."

"A what?"

"A Prince Albert. Named for one of Queen Victoria's son's. It's penile mutilation of a sort. A ring through the foreskin. It went out of fashion as circumcision came into vogue, now its back." He thought a moment. "You know, it must be interesting to have that extra sensation added to the act."

"Maybe. Unfortunately you don't have the proper equipment." JB could feel his balls scrunch up at the very thought of such a procedure. And that remark? He'd slept long enough with Len when they were going together to know he was cut. "But look here, Len, this man's barbell is a custom job. One of the two balls is bigger than the other..."

"Ah, just like you," Len chuckled, getting his own dig in.

JB bent to look closer at Matty's chest. "...and the larger ball has some sort of gold inlay on it. Some fancy scroll work. That's not your run of the mill nipple bar. That's a custom job."

The staff member, who was standing next to JB and Len wrote what was being said on the card he was holding, while also crossing out the dead man's fake name and writing in the correct one. "I've got to tell the police about this." he said, then asked JB, "Will you watch the room to make sure nothing is disturbed?"

"Sure. But I doubt anyone will want to go in there. It's pretty ghastly."

JB looked around, noticing that the other gathered patrons, at the mention of the police, had silently retreated back to their own rooms. There was just himself, Len, and the staff guy standing in the hallway now.

The staff guy said to JB, "I won't be long." Then he pointed to Henry still lying in the room. "If he comes to, don't let him go anywhere. The cops will definitely want to talk to him." With that he went running off back to the office.

"So, what do you think?" Len was swinging a finger between the dead man and the passed out guy. "Did Henry there go into Matty's room and defend the honor of Miz' Dimity by shooting her manager in the puss?"

"I suppose that's a plausible explanation."

"Puss? Isn't that a great word for a private detective to use?"

"Not unless it's Nineteen-thirty-five." JB tapped his chin with his finger. "You know, this could be rough sex gone very very bad" He paused. "Then again, I could be barking up the proverbial wrong tree. There could be multiple reasons for this."

"How is rough sex wrong? Is that some sort of gay slur, JB?"

"Of course not. I'm a great believer in whatever gets your boat to shore. You know, I read that someone is murdered in New York City every eighteen hours. And, trust me, there are way more than eighteen reasons for every one of the dead."

"Uh oh. You have that look on your face again."

"What look?" JB stood a little taller and slid a hand along the side of his head. "Oh, I know, you mean my GQ model look, don't you?"

"No. I mean your Nancy Drew is on the case look."

"Oh. Well, you could be right about that. I already have several questions."

"Well, crap, there goes the rest of the night." Len was not the least bit surprised at how willing he was to accept JB's intervention into what should have been strictly a police matter. He might have been taken aback five of JB's novels ago but not anymore. "Okay, Inspector Clouseau, what questions are we asking?"

"For one, why is Henry there still in the room? If you'd just shot someone wouldn't you haul ass away from the scene of the crime? And why is he passed out? That makes no sense at all. Unless..."

Henry, the piano player, chose this moment to come out of his coma. His eyes flickered open; he shivered as if cold and shook his head then sat up with a moan. A hand went to the back of his neck. Groggy, he tripped over the words he was attempting to say. "What happened?" was about as close as he got too coherent.

Len bent down to feel at Henry's forehead, then silently pointed to the bed. Henry's eyes followed Len's finger. He started and whispered, "What the fu..." He grabbed Len's arm, "Who is that?"

JB, instantly going into a Sam Spade interrogation mode—Len's earlier remark had gotten him thinking about the 1930's—asked Henry, "You don't know who that is? Then why were you in his room? And holding a gun?"

Henry looked down dumbly at his hand. Seeing the gun lying in it, he jerked it away, letting the weapon clatter onto the floor. In a voice gone to a squeak, he choked out, "That's not mine. I don't know where it came from." Realization of the circumstances he was in then made his eyes go wide with fright. His head started to shake uncontrollably. "No. No. No. I didn't...I wouldn't...I didn't kill him. I couldn't have. Who is that?

I don't know him, I swear. I guarantee you that I..." He almost screamed the end of his sentence. "...I didn't kill anyone."

Len, taking charge, took one of Henry's arms and helped him to stand. In an incongruously cheerful voice, he said to Henry, "Why don't we move you down to the bar, old boy? They have water there...we can clean up that blood on your neck."

Henry reached again for his head. His eyes widened when he saw the blood smeared on his fingers. "I'm hurt. How'd that happen? This is insane."

As Len guided Henry passed JB, he softly said to his friend, "We don't want him contaminating your little crime scene, now do we?" And he winked.

JB stood stiff from surprise. His head was tilted slightly off-kilter. "No, I-I guess not," he stammered. Watching after Len with some puzzlement he stepped over to the unhinged door, took hold of it, and moved it so it was propped across the opening—effectively covering the dead man from anyone's view.

Still staring after Len, JB wondered where the hell Len was getting this sudden command of the language of detection. Contaminating the crime scene? How had Len Matthews, major silly queen, taken in the room, quickly surmised what any self-respecting investigator might have seen, and handling the situation with some previously unknown expertise, had done exactly the right thing? What's going on here? This is not what anyone expected from Len Matthews. He was the one that always would take it too far—and then be very pleased that he had.

JB, still somewhat bemused by Len's actions, followed him down the hall. Len was leading the injured Henry down the stairs.

"You've done it again, Len."

"What have I done now, JB?"

"You've done exactly the right thing in a situation fraught with opportunity to go wrong. I am quite amazed..."

"And, you know what else, JB. I'm getting damn tired of you underestimating my ability to handle myself in a crisis. I'm no dummy, you know. So cut it out."

JB held up his hands. "Okay. So, you're way tougher than I thought you were..."

"I am tough, damn it. So tough I'm thinking of getting my eyelids tattooed. How about that?"

JB laughed at the absurdity of his suggestion. "With what, pray tell?"

"The word 'You' on the right lid. Now take a wild guess what I have in mind for the left."

"Tsk. Tsk." JB shook his head. "Language, Len."

"It's good old street vernacular English. Why?"

"And that's another thing. Where has this sudden command of the language come from? You don't usually play around with words. Unless they're your part in a script. What's up?"

"If you must know I've received an offer to write a book from a publisher..."

JB stopped on the stairs. There wasn't one word Len had just said that didn't have a question attached to it. "You've what?" JB was to say the least taken by a great degree of surprise at Len's news. As far as he was aware what Len knew about writing a book could be written in capital letters with a blunt pencil on a mosquitoes ass.

Len helped Henry to sit on the stair riser and turned back to face JB. "You paused for a moment there. I know you, Jeremy Bent You have something to say about the offer, don't you? Come on, out with it."

JB wasn't exactly sure what he was supposed to say about this turn of events. At first glance it seemed a nice piece of publicity for Len, and JB should be happy for his friend. However, on second glance, JB was wondering what the hell Len was thinking. JB was the writer in their duo, not Len. He was the one who'd made his name in the book trade, not Len. Len was always the more public figure, the one who struts upon a stage and performs his little acts. JB was the thinker, the tinkerer of language. And, on the third and fourth glance, Len wasn't supposed to be stomping around in JB's personal territory, damn it.

Then JB didn't really want to seem that

small and petty now did he? He decided to use a dodge. Evasion was always a winning maneuver in these situations. "No, no, Len. I couldn't possibly have an opinion until I've read something you've written. You have written something, haven't you? A short story. An article? A grocery list? I mean really, Len, a book? What kind are we talking about here? Fiction? Nonfiction? Travelogue? Gossip?" He stepped down to stand evenly with Len on the stairs.

Len was looking a little uncomfortable. "It's supposed to be the true and unvarnished story of my life...so far."

"Ah." JB was relieved. It wasn't so much of a much after all. "You're talking about biography as fiction then? Like Liberace's most recent autobiography. He had the nerve to say that Sonia Henie was the love of his life? Really? What about all those boys that followed him around everywhere? I mean, there's a lot you couldn't really talk about isn't there? Do you really think a book is a good idea, Len?"

"What? I would be telling the truth? It would be a bestseller I bet?"

"So you'd go ahead and tell the whole world about yourself? You'd come out as gay in print? Tell the entire world that you're a great big Mo? What would that do to your career?"

"It might invigorate it. I'm getting tired of slaving away for no money on Broadway. A bit of notoriety might bump up my price. Get me known. Get me offers."

"Slaves don't make the kind of money you're making, Len. You manage on a leading man's salary of thousands every week. You do all right."

"Oh, sure, I get by, but I can't tell you how many actor friends I know who are making real killings in film and on television. Do you have any idea the perks you get doing a TV series? I wouldn't mind some of that big-time cash coming my way. It wouldn't hurt to built up my share of the FU money. Besides, there are some actors who are out now. How about Ian McKellen? Everybody knows he's gay."

"But he's still not public about it. Neither is Nathan

Lane, or any number of other actors we know. And what is FU money?"

"Well, maybe its time one of us does come out to the public. And FU means exactly what you think it means. Money socked away so I can say exactly that to crummy scripts and bad shows."

Henry, who had been leaning against the balustrade on the stairway, moaned. Len bent to check on him.

"Are you hanging in there, Henry?" Len turned back to JB. "Good God, don't you get it? The AIDS crisis and the outright fear that the disease engenders in the public are decimating our whole community. Don't you see JB? How can the straights be afraid of somebody they know personally? Maybe its time there's another gay besides Rock Hudson. Come on, they all know about me. It isn't all that much of a secret anyway."

"So, you're seriously thinking of doing this?"

Len bent and hefted Henry to a position at his side. "We need to get Henry downstairs, JB. Come on." Len started down the stairs again, saying back to JB. "I haven't signed any book contracts yet so you shouldn't panic over this. There haven't been any major decisions made, and I probably won't be coming out in print anytime soon. We can discuss this later. Okay? Hell, I'm not even sure I could write a book."

JB followed him. "So you'll get a ghostwriter then?"

"I don't know about that? Do you know how much they cost? Humm, maybe I could write a book. Its not that far fetched. You're not the only one that likes playing around with the English language."

"True. And they say everyone has a book in them. I just happened to have six or seven. So far. I do tend to rack up points on the scoreboard in that arena more often than you."

# VI

The three of them arrived at the bar. Len waved a hand to get the attention of the bartender. He came over to see what was the matter. Was the man Len was holding drunk or hurt? Indicating Henry, he asked, "Is he okay? Is there something wrong?"

"He needs a drink," Len said, as he helped Henry to sit on one of the stools. "Bourbon, please."

"Mixed with?"

"Just pour it, Brian. And hurry, please. He can mix it in his mouth."

Len bent to look into the man's very glassy eyes. They had stopped spinning in their sockets by now, but were headed directly toward shock. They were going in and out of focus. Not a good sign. Len was guessing that a drink should help. It always did him.

He looked up when Brian set the shot down in front of their wounded victim. Len picked it up and force fed the amber liquid down Henry's throat, pouring it as if Henry's mouth was an open yaw.

Henry tried to swallow but his yaw too soon filled and whiskey began to slosh out over his lips and chin. Too much for him he sputtered, spraying Len with the liquor. Len sighed. It had been awhile since he'd smelled the oaky aroma of distilled spirits. It was actually quite pleasant without that extra barf smell that had previously accompanied most of his drinking. Henry slapped at his chest trying to get a breath. Len took to pounding on his back to help.

JB, who had watched this as if it were a slapstick movie sthick, took a seat facing Henry and said, "I think you're going to be all right? However, we do have quite a few questions to ask. About your being in that room first of all."

Henry still couldn't speak so he simply waved a hand at JB to stall him. Len asked Brian for a glass of water, which Henry gulped down to clear his throat and get his voice back. Finally he said, "I don't remember anything. I know I went up to the room. I was going there to talk with Matty. But I didn't have a gun with me. I wasn't going to hurt him. That wasn't what I meant at all."

Brian the bartender handed a damp towel to Len so he could wipe at the drops of whiskey Henry had spewed over him. That done he then used the towel to wipe at the blood on Henry's neck and to check it for the amount of damage. What he found was a small cut, the type that bleeds profusely but isn't nearly as bad as it appears.

Brian the bartender, still standing across from them, coughed. Len looked over. "Yes, okay, I know you're there. But I'm going to ask if we can't put our conversation off for a little bit. I'm sort of busy right this minute. But, I do want to talk with you. Okay?" Brian the bartender nodded and went off to the other end of the bar to attend to another customer.

The voice asking "What's going on, Henry?" was neither JB's nor Len's. The question being asked was coming from a sleepy eyed and disheveled Dimity London, the singer from the cabaret act, standing at the other end of the bar. She had a rhinestone encrusted eye mask shoved up on her forehead, her platinum blond hair was tangled and tousled about her head. One hand was stifling a yawn, while the other was gripping closed the same chenille robe she had been wearing when they'd last seen her.

JB swung around to face her. "Better yet, Ms. London, I should ask you what are you doing in a men's bathhouse at two-fifteen AM in the morning? Also, you definitely know this man is Henry Lavender? You can identify him." JB could get officially stuffy on occasion.

She answered him in a voice filled with bluster and false bravado. "Of course that's Henry," she said. "He's only played piano for me for three years." The woman had a speaking voice of a timbre not heard since Ethel Merman stomped along Broadway and Times Square. It was all on one note. Loud. She took a step toward them, and spoke to Henry. "Are you all right, honey? Have these men been molesting you?"

"Considering that's the whole point of the bath's existence that's a very naive question, Ms. London." Len would get huffy at the odd moment himself.

JB took over. "If you must know we're helping Henry out until the police arrive. They'll want to talk with him."

"I don't get it. Why are the police coming here? Talk to him about what?" Her stance took on a combative pose. Feet spread wide with belligerence, her hands knotted into fists. "What's going on here?"

"There's been a murder here tonight and Henry may have been involved. Does that answer your question?" She nodded, backing down only a smidge. "Then will you answer mine, please? What exactly are you doing here?" JB could be as blunt as she was being.

She ran sharp nails through her hair, pushing it back behind an ear. "I took a nap after the show. I must have slept longer than I thought. What do you mean a murder? Was that the noise that woke me."

The lady was the type that wanted answer's right away. Without any folderol or fancy curly-cues attached. She was as tough as an aged queen's A-hole. No pissey little extra millimeter girly smokes for her. No drinks with fruit. No darling handbags. No sandlewood soaps. None of that pussy shit. She was what 1950's mystery writers would have called a broad. A doll. A bowzer.

JB looked at the clock over the bar. "And it took you an hour to investigate? Why so long?"

"I heard the noise, but I didn't connect it with a real gunshot. I was thinking it was a firecracker or something. So I turned back over. Why are you asking me this? I didn't have nothing to do with no murder."

"Didn't you, Ms. London? Since the dead man is someone you knew pretty well you would have as good a reason to kill him as Henry. Why couldn't you have killed him? Henry has been saying he didn't do it."

Dimity patted her chest. "And he's blaming me?" She turned to face him. "How could you, you son-of-a-bitch?"

Henry waved his hand in protest. "No. No. I've only been saying it wasn't me. I haven't blamed anyone else." He turned to face JB. "And don't you say I did."

Jeez, touchy these folk, aren't they? He asked himself, why is that? JB went on, "Then logic tells us it has to be somebody other than Henry who murdered the guy. Who else would have a reason to kill him other than someone who knew him? Someone who'd had a argument with him earlier in the evening?"

"Who the hell are you talking about? Who got killed?"

Len was surprised at her question. "You don't know?"

Her head swung a denial.

"The dead man was your manager. Matty Silverman. That's who's lying upstairs...murdered. With a bloody pulp where his face used to be." Len had put the facts out in the most macabre fashion he could. He knew JB would be as interested in seeing her reaction as much as he was.

Dimity's face first registered pure shock. As if she'd been struck by a bolt of thunder. "What? Matty? No," she gasped. Her hands ran through her hair, she went pale, moaned, and fainted.

# VII

Meanwhile, over at the front window, the clerk was checking in a new customer from the line that had formed out in the lobby. Currently checking in was a little man with a partly smoked unfiltered cigarette hanging off his lower lip. He was dressed in a long dark overcoat with remnants of ashes and gray smudges flecking the front. He was signing in as Chester A. Arthur. Over one of his shoulders he carried a black fabric sided suitcase. Unbeknownst to the uninterested clerk the suitcase held a professional camera and all its various accessories and not the sex toys most would have thought it did.

The man signing in as Mr. Arthur was a member of a band of feral-like photographers that spend their lives dogging celebrities around the city. The reason was so they could sell their ill-gotten photos of the famous to the *New York Post* or any of the other tabloid papers in town. He was a member of a band of miscreants that would prefer to call themselves stringers.

They are probably better known as the paparazzi —named after their equivalent operating in Rome, Italy in the 1950's when the cinema there was producing stars such as Sophia Loren, Verna Lisi, and Gina Lollobrigida. Paparazzi were packs of camera wielding reporters who took candid and scandalous pictures of the well and wannabe well known. The people they follow and harass have many more colorful names for them.

This particular paparazzo's reason for checking into the baths was because he'd been listening to police calls on his car radio scanner earlier that evening. When he'd heard that a police homicide unit was being requested at Aesop's Atrium he knew he had to follow up on it. Exactly what he was getting into he didn't know, but he did know it had to be juicy if it involved a gay bathhouse.

Signed in after him were Alfred E. Newman, Carter Milktoast, Mayor Koch, and Barbara Stanwyck.

It was ten minutes later when JB heard, "What the hell!" A man's voice boomed from the outer hall. Loud enough so it was heard all the way inside. The voice was high pitched, sounding like Tweetybird was royally pissed, and it pinged and echoed off the tiled walls like a mockingbirds call. It yelled, "You're shitting me, right? You've been letting random people into my crime scene?"

The clerk in his box stammered back. "But, officer, nobody told me different. I didn't know I wasn't..."

JB first ticked to the voice using the term crime scene. He quickly realized, the police must have arrived. And to top it off JB was finding that irritated voice he was hearing sounding vaguely familiar. He listened closer. There was something about the agitato of it.

"I don't friggin' believe it," it was shouting. "I want them all found. Anyone you've let in since we were called. I want them brought right here to the lobby. Everyone of them. And now, damn it."

The clerk, cowed by the officer's tone, stuttered back, "Bu, but, how? How am I supposed to find them?"

"I don't care. Just do it."

JB looked over at Len and said, "It looks like the cops have arrived. And, weirdly enough, I think I know which cop it is." JB took hold of Len's shoulders. "Do me a favor. Can you keep the cops busy down here while I run upstairs and take another look at the room with the body. I want to check it out before the forensic guys get in there. They'll just mess it all up with their ham fisted methods. Can you do that for me?"

"I suppose. But isn't this you sticking your nose in where it won't be welcomed?"

"You know as well as I do that the police are only trained to miss the point. They'll just get it all wrong. They always have before. What I'm really doing here is picking up where the law leaves off. I won't be long." He turned and ran up the stairs.

Len pasted on one of his more winning smiles and waited for the officer they'd heard yelling outside to come inside.

He did a few moments later. Followed closely by another officer. This one in uniform. A very handsome uniform at that Len noticed. Expertly tailored and draped on rather a fine young and hot body. That certainly got his interest up.

More than a few men in uniform could be attractive to Len's epicene sensibilities. Not all, of course. Herman Goring for example. He was bratwurst stuffed in a too tight casing. Not a pretty picture. On the other hand, this young man wearing a NYC duty uniform was very pretty indeed. His hats patent leather brim and the gold badge with the sergeants stripes on his sleeve was enough for Len to feel himself coming to attention already. Why is it that we men can always be led around so mindlessly by our dicks? That member fills with blood and a man's brain simply ceases to function normally. Highly inconvenient at times—it's hell when a tube of flesh becomes the one who must be obeyed.

The shorter of the two cops, the one obviously in charge, spoke to Len first. "My name is Detective Kelly," he said in a voice an octave too high for the man he presented himself as. He sounded as if he'd been sucking on helium or was a member of the Lollypop Guild.

Len almost let a derisive snort escape. But realizing that one of those would certainly irritate the officer he held it in. Instead he took an appraisal of the man himself. Humm, despite that voice he was very attractive. Of Irish origin, which was obvious from a full head of burnt red wavy hair and a smattering of freckles across his pug nose. Built somewhat like a pug too, with a thick chest, narrow waist, and his head set peevishly on broad shoulders. What he wasn't was tall. He only came up to Len's shoulders. He pointed a hand at his partner. "This is Sergeant Hampton."

Len grinned at the pretty policeman. "Ah, like the Long Island Hamptons? I've spent some wonderful weekends out there. At Tony Perkin's place. Beautiful home, right on the wa..."

"Uh-hmm," Detective Kelly grunted. "Can we get on with this? There's been a murder reported here tonight. What do you know about it...uh...Mister?"

Then, before Len could even answer, Kelly turned to his sergeant and said, "Roger, I need you to go out and patrol the lobby for me. Make sure that clerk doesn't let in any more people. And take charge of the ones he rounds up. Okay?"

The sergeant nodded and turned to leave, but not without miming one of those 'why are you doing this to me' looks at the detective. Could there be trouble in the ranks, Len wondered?

The detective turned back to Len and gave him an "excuse me" shrug, then went after the sergeant to talk with him.

Len gave a shrug of his own and went to the bar to sit with Henry, while quietly watching the detective and his sergeant have their conversation.

The body language between them told Len just

about everything he needed to know about the dynamic between the two men. He had seen one or two lovers have quarrels before, so he could guess the pretty uniformed cop and the handsome detective were somewhere in the throes of an affair. Workplace sex, huh? And the affair not going all that well at the moment it would seem. Humm, a gay cop and his boyfriend working the same case. How cute. How complicated.

Len turned to the bar. Standing directly across from him was Brian the bartender again. Speaking of complications. He's waiting to have that talk. Len sighed. "Yes, Brian. We'll talk. I promise. But again, not now. Can we do it later please."

Len knew he going to have to have this conversation with Brian. He just needed a little while to figure what he was going to say. How to make what needed to be said a little less uncomfortable for himself.

# VIII

t took JB only a minute to shift the door he had placed over the cubicle's opening. The body was still there—unmoving, still, cold. There's something discomfiting about the silence that follows death. The absence of life hangs heavily in the air.

JB shivered a bit and crossed his arms over his chest as protection from the Reaper's grasp. It also prevented him from leaving any of his fingerprints where they might not belong. The one thing he didn't need was to become a suspect in the case.

To be honest he wasn't even sure what he was looking for in the little room, but Henry's vehement denials had been enough to persuade him to take a second look around. There wasn't a whole hell of a lot to see.

Since the dead man was in the altogether, without even one of the regulation issued towels to cover his privates there weren't any pockets to look through. So that avenue of investigation was useless. What else was there?

Hanging on the three hooks against the wall were the

dead man's few pieces of clothing.

According to the labels there was a relatively expensive Brooks Brothers suit jacket and matching trousers, a Bill Blass white on white striped dress shirt with a monogrammed pocket, and a pair of boxer shorts festooned with tiny flying ducks. JB could never get why men persisted in the wearing of boxer shorts. Having your privates shifting and flopping around your crotch all day would be annoying at best. Plus all that fabric crawling up your ass crack was simply weird.

JB turned to look at the dead man. He noticed that his watch was gone. The bracelet he'd been wearing when JB had last seen him was now missing from his wrist. Then was robbery a reason for his killer coming to the cubicle? It didn't seem likely since a ring with a good sized stone was still on the dead man's finger, and there was a nice sized diamond stud in his left ear. Plus the gold and silver nipple bar on his teat was still there.

Then robbery couldn't be the motive here? Interesting? Did the watch have some meaning to whoever it was that had done this? It was a distinct possibility. What that significance might be JB couldn't possibly know at this juncture. That piece of information would have to come out of further investigation.

JB was asking these questions because he'd decided he really didn't believe Henry was the murderer they were looking for. Henry being found in the condition he was in raised a red flag too many. Knocked out cold with a gun in his hand was simply too easy. It was almost theatrical in its perfection. For JB it had the look and feel of a staged set. It had become clear to him that Henry was being set up to appear the killer.

The light in the room was dim, so JB reached over and turned the rheostat switch up to high. The brightness increased and JB was better able to see what was what. What was there in the tiny room that might have some relevance to the questions JB was forming about the crime?

What jumped out at him was the dead man's

right hand. It sat elegantly on his lap—as if it had been posed to be so artistic. It looked to JB as if the hand was holding something out. Perhaps a bouquet for some unknown beau?

Of course, in the baths protocol would have it that any open door was an invitation to accept a trick into your space. In that case Matty's hand held out so cunningly could have held several things—a dildo, a whip, any number of accouterments could have been used as invitation into his space. Meaning his fingers being held just so only said they could have been gripped around something that had nothing to do with his being killed. Gay men could be up to all kinds of profligate and debauched doings of an evening at the tubs. Enough so even the Marquise deSade would have been impressed with their inventiveness. What our dead man may have been holding in his hand was now missing. His hand was held in a gesture that would never be fulfilled.

JB then noticed another something about his hand. He bent in to get a closer look. That was odd? The nailbeds of the dead man's fingers had discolored in death. The color was pale, but definitely blue. Could that be cyanosis of his fingers?

JB stood and scratched the back of his neck. That itch was his alarm system going off. When something didn't fit, when something weird was standing out on an investigation, the back of his neck would start to tingle.

Well, that makes no sense at all, JB was thinking. Blue tinged nails are a symptom of a completely different way of dying. Of cardiopulmonary arrest or poison or an overdose of drugs. Matty had a gunshot wound. Then where did that discoloration come from?

If there was poison present—and at this point it was a large if—what was the gunshot to his face about? Poison would have made the gun blast they'd heard totally unnecessary? Why would a killer shoot a man who was already dead from taking poison? In the end, JB realized, it would take the coroners report to verify that there was a poison even present, so that line of questions would have to wait a bit.

JB went on to rifle through the few remaining article's of Matty's clothing. There was little except pocket lint. What he was hoping for was something to explain the why of Matty Silverman's death. A note. An address. A matchbook with a phone number. Anything that would provide a lead to what had happened in this little room. JB found nothing. Even so there were still a few things to be found out about the dead man.

For instance, JB could make a guess as to what type of hygiene Matty practiced. He reached for the duck shorts. As idiotic as it sounded you could actually tell a lot from a man's crotch. Was the victim OCD about his smells? Or was he into the grunge scene. There were men JB knew who were turned on by the smell of a raunchy unwashed crotch. Not something he was crazy about himself but everybody to their own fetish, right?

Gross odor wasn't the case when JB put the fly of the boxers against his nose. What he got was a whiff of talc with an under sniff of lavender. So, Matty Silverman had good hygiene.

"What the hell...?"

There was that familiar voice again. It was the voice JB had heard downstairs, but clearer now that it was coming from directly behind him. It was interesting. High in tone but still masculine. A mellow tenor JB would call it. Perfect for singing Irish laments about "muthers", but without the lilt and the accent. Truman Capote without the prissy affectations.

JB stopped cold where he stood, his nose stuck in the dead man's underwear. Oh, oh, this won't look good at all. His mind raced. Len must have been unable to keep the police down at the bar, because that voice coming from behind him sounded very much like his old friend Captain Colin Kelly.

Captain Kelly had been JB's collaborator on a couple of the cases that he'd worked on. Cases that had led directly to JB writing the first two books in his series.****

****Those two novels would be *Secret's Don't Belong In Closets* and *A Murderous Ball Of Fluff.*

He had always regarded the policeman in a benevolent and friendly light. Captain Kelly might not have been quite so generous with his own description of JB. His opinion, according to an interview given at the time, was far more scathing and uncomplimentary. Captain Kelly was prone to using language to describe JB that his mother would have washed his mouth with soap for.

The voice JB was now hearing had exactly the same gruff timbre as his Captain Kelly. Filled to overflowing with the authority given it by the New York City Police Department, Homicide Division.

Right then the voice was asking a very accusatory, "Finding anything interesting there are you?"

This was said with the same mocking tone that gay men will use when they turn something innocent into something salacious. For instance an innocuous "There's a trash basket behind the bar..." would be turned by adding "...and it's usually the bartender." That sort of thing.

JB put as charming a smile as he was able onto his face and spun to greet the officer, planning to use as much flimflam on the Captain as he could muster in the moment. Expecting to see the virulently bulldog face of his Captain Kelly was one thing. What he found was something else all together.

The figure standing in front of him was much younger than his Kelly. And way better looking. "Uh... Oh, sorry...Ha...I thought you were somebody else..." Further word's withered at the back of JB's throat.

There was a completely unknown person standing in the doorway, watching him with quite nice but narrowed and suspicious eyes. Where JB's Kelly had been described by his fellow officers as "grim," and his manner that of a pissed off bulldog, this person in front of JB would be considered absolutely fine by any set of standards. He could even serve as the model of what a policeman should look like. This man was poster-boy material.

He was square jawed, with a finely turned up nose and the hint of a cleft at the chin. Dick Tracy stepped out of the comic pages. TV's Remington Steele come to life. The man wasn't all that tall—the top of his head stopped right at JB's shoulder—so calling him bantam sized would be kind. He was around thirty—young for a plainclothes detective—and very nicely proportioned. He had what looked to be an athletic build confined in a well-tailored gray suit with a brightly patterned tie.

The tie was one that JB had seen for sale at the MoMA Design Shop a few weeks previously when he had viewed the museum's exhibit on the history of ergonomic office chairs. The tie had an abstract paisley design in pinks, greens with a splash of orange. Kooky. Fun. Meaning the cop had, at the least, some taste—and a nicely developed sense of humor. JB decided there was a young Jimmy Cagney vibe about him. Hadn't Cagney played an early G-man role in one of his Warner Brother's movies? This cop came on like that. Not that he looked anything like the 1930's actor. He only gave off the same sort of energy. Save for a head of wavy russet hair and knowing droll eyes he didn't look much like Cagney at all. His features were softer; more refined, nowhere near as belligerent and cocky as Cagney's had been. This one wasn't a rooster. More of a dove with a stubborn streak.

"...You sounded just like another cop I know," JB went on. "But he's much older than you are. And from a different precinct I'll bet. You wouldn't know him by any chance? His name is Kelly? Colin Kelly. Captain Kelly that is..." JB chuckled nervously as he leaned forward to read the name badge pinned to the cop's coat pocket. "Hey...I'll be damned, your name is Kelly too. How's that possible?"

What the hell? Why couldn't he just shut the hell up? If the hole he was digging in front of this man got any deeper he'd find a rice paddy.

The cop smiled. It was charming, and tipped his face over to truly handsome. "Colin Kelly? Sure. I know him. He's my uncle. I'm Liam. Liam Kelly. And you are?" He held out a hand.

JB stepped forward and grabbed at it to shake it, then realized it held the cop's ID and badge. "Oh." His hand went limp. "I'm Jeremy Bent. I was..."

The cop interrupted, "You're that writer guy? I've heard about you. From Uncle Colin, of course. And I read a couple of your books."

JB replied with a knowing smile, "Yeah? I'm sure Captain Kelly had plenty to say about me. But I'll bet you can't prove any of it?"

"I don't know, he only said you'd worked with him to solve a murder case or two."

"And that's all? In that case I'm very glad to meet you, Officer Kelly."

"Detective Kelly. Or better yet, why don't you call me Liam. Should I call you Jeremy?"

"JB. Please call me JB. All my friends do."

The detective leaned over like a Rock-Em Sock-Em blow up figure to look past JB. "So, you've checked out this crime scene here. What did you find if I might ask? Anything of value? Anything I can use?"

JB was flattered that he would ask. Cops weren't usually so open to an outside interloper giving their opinions.

JB spun around to look at the victim. "Well, rigor mortis hasn't set in yet, and his eyelids are still flaccid, so I'd put death within the hour. But, there are some questions I have that might bring any simple murder theory into question."

The cop asked, "Such as?"

JB went on to point out the blue tinged fingers on the dead man hands and then mentioned the lack of motive on Henry's part. JB was enjoying himself, having the floor to himself, when the cop stopped him. He said, "Then your supposing that someone other than the guy downstairs was involved in this?"

"That's it. Exactly. But, if that is the case..."

And the two detectives were off and riding on an investigative riff together. Finding their individual theories expressed and verbalized between them, laid out neatly for examination by the other. Then the two men would piggyback on that, which would lead to more ideas and theories about the crime at hand. Discovering more reasons for gunfire in the middle of the night. More reasons for naked bodies found in tiny rooms.

This cop—like magic JB felt—had somehow managed to connect with him. As if the officer had turned onto JB's track, bought a ticket, and jumped on board for the ride. Detective Liam Kelly had become to JB what Watson was to Holmes, Number One Son to Chan. They were each using their insights to launch them to possibilities other than simply A shooting B in a cubical at the baths.

JB was saying, "So, possible motives for most murders tend to be..." He ticked them off on his fingers. "...profit, revenge, jealousy, concealment of a crime, avoiding humiliation, or plain homicidal mania. It's all there on page one of the murder manual. Which one of the people here tonight is the cause of this murder is up for grabs. It could be any one of them."

JB had replaced the door over the opening and the two men were walking down the stairs toward the bar. Waiting there was Henry Lavender, the policeman's current suspect.

To JB it seemed that even if the detective did talk to Henry, his being the main suspect had to be in serious doubt by what JB had offered. That wasn't such a bad thing, but it did mean there would have be more investigating done before the case was finally solved. It was clear there was more to this shooting than a gun firing off on a Tuesday night at the tubs.

And it was right there, without JB even meaning it to happen, that he found himself once again drawn into figuring out what that was. How did this keep happening to him? Before long he was going to start losing all his friends, since there is nothing that will put a damper on a conversation like discussing your latest murder case. That's why people would run when Jessica Fletcher walked into a room.

# IX

At the entrance to the bar area the detective left JB to head off to where Henry was sitting. The officer was eager to begin his interrogation of his single suspect. JB, instead of joining him, aimed for Dimity London, who was sitting at the other end of the bar. JB didn't need to be a party to Henry's interrogation since he was already familiar with what Henry had to say from the earlier protests of his innocence.

Henry had repeatedly said all he remembered was that he had gone to Matty's cubical to confront him over his ill treatment of Dimity. That was his explanation for why he was upstairs. He said he had knocked on the door frame and stepped into the room. After that it was all a blank until he woke up with Len leaning over him and an egg sized bump on the back of his head.

JB concluded there had to be another someone in that room. Whoever that person was had smacked Henry upside the cranium and knocked him out cold. Then the same person had tried to incriminate Henry in the shooting by leaving a gun in his hand.

Henry's story had a ring of truth to it for JB. It also

went a long way toward explaining why Henry was still in the room when Silverman's body was found. What JB wasn't so sure about was what these three people were to each other. Matty and Dimity London, Dimity and Henry, Henry and Matty. Maybe Dimity could fill in some of the blank spots in the trio's confusing relationships.

Having hung around Len Matthews for as many years as JB had it was inevitable that some of his more genteel Southern manners would have rubbed off. JB stepped up to where Dimity was sitting and said, "Excuse me, ma'am, but may I ask you a few questions?"

Dimity, who was raised in Queens and now lived in Brooklyn, wasn't having it. "Sure, bub. Whatta' you wanna' know?" Her manner was brusque, straight from the gut. "Call me Dimity, bub. I ain't no madam, ya see. I'm no murderer either, as you intimated I was earlier."

JB put on his most genial smile, "I have to apologize for that..."—not because you didn't have motive, JB was thinking—"...but the logistics of a woman sneaking around a men's bathhouse in the middle of the night just doesn't work for me. So I have to believe you're not a suspect in that regard. What I did want to ask you about was your relationship with Mr. Silverman. I mean, from what I could tell it seemed...uh...antagonistic at best."

That's when Dimity's hard candy shell cracked open and the gooey nougat was exposed. "Oh, no," she fluttered. "You don't understand." She seemed distraught, almost in tears. "Matty was like a brother to me." She wiped at an eye. "Officially, he was my agent, but we've been through so much together we were the same as family to each other. There was nothing salacious about it, you understand." She sniffed. "I did have a crush on him early on, but it turned out he was gay. So we entered the friend zone. Matty and I."

"What zone?"

"Friend. Where there's no chance of anyone getting

together in a nether-regional way. It wasn't general knowledge, but Matty had a long term boyfriend. Erik's uncle, if you must know."

"Erik? Who's that?"

"Erik. My male backup singer? See. That's what I was talking about. We're all family."

"Ah, I know who you mean. The GQ magazine gorgeous one, right? Is he available for dating?"

"Not with you, sweetheart. He's not of the Tinkerbell persuasion. He's straight."

"Is he really? Then why is he coming out of the steam room over there?"

JB pointed over to the very naked man just stepping out of the steam room door. A cloud of white fog followed and swirled around him, making his exit into a kind of Renaissance archangelic tableau. Narcissus rising from the sea. He casually wrapped his towel at his waist and sauntered off in the direction of the TV room.

# X

Dimity's screech echoed in the tiled enclosure of the bathhouse. "Erik!!!!! What the fuccckk!!" Erik acted exactly as any startled animal would. He stood stark still while his eyes frantically sought the source of the sound. Seeing it was Dimity who'd beckoned, he scurried, quick like a bunny, skipping around the central pit and into the bar. He sidled up next to Dimity and asked—in what JB could plainly hear was a very nervous tone—"Ha. Uh, what are you doing here, sweetie?"

"Outing you, apparently," she answered with a sniff. She was obviously building up to a right royal snit. "So, if you're a homo what's this shit about you banging Iris?" She leaned back toward JB and explained, "That's one of my other backup singers. The lanky platinum blond that looks like a drag queen. Not the one with the legs that go to Chicago and back. He was supposed to be shtuping her." She swung back to face Erik. A peevish mean grimace slanted her mouth. "So, come on, fess up. Are you a one of these gay boys, Erik? Do you bash the shuttlecock from the feathered end?"

"No, no," Erik stammered. "I'm no queer, Dimity. You know that." His voice had taken on the same tone used by a three year old when caught with crummy hands in cookie jars. "Nothing was going on in there. Really. Ah, come on, Dimity, I'm straight. You have to understand." He reached for a plausible excuse. Any excuse would do. "I–I stayed tonight for the steam. Yeah...For my back." He began to rub at his right side, while he pasted on what he must have hoped was an ingratiating truthful looking smile. "I have this arthritis of the spine, you see." He was still whining but had an expression he must have thought made him look angelic and truthful.

It looked to JB more like a case of trying too hard. The only part missing was him knee-bent and pleading for the lady's forgiveness. JB took a guess that Dimity must rule her employee's with an iron fist in a steel glove. That is if Erik's reaction to his employer's questions was any indication. JB wondered what the benefits had to be for him to put up with this sort of treatment. "I can bring a doctor's note if you need one," Erik ended on a hopeful note. It was too much excuse, not enough veracity.

JB was also coming to the rather surprising conclusion that even the facially blessed, as Erik certainly was, can have their problems. If his desperate story was anywhere close too true, being perfect looking didn't make for perfect living. Poor baby, JB was thinking—which was probably the exact reaction Erik was hoping for.

There was more salubrious whining on Erik's part which JB finally just stopped paying attention to. He began to focus on and scan the lobby. Trying out another of the arrows in any detective's quiver. Observation.

He wanted to see exactly who would be the next person out of the steamroom Erik had just left. It might give him some indication of what had really been going on inside there. It wasn't as if he didn't already have a pretty good idea, despite Erik's claims otherwise. Of course it was only an assumption on JB's part, but experience told him that ducks walked like ducks and people who patronized gay bathhouses were usually gay, and there was both hanky and panky going on somewhere nearby.

The frosted door of the steamroom opened and who should step out but Len, wrapped in nothing but his towel and a rather pleased expression on his face.

JB stood up from the bar to go meet him, which left Dimity and Erik to thrash out their problem on their own. Whatever the dynamic between them, it really didn't concern him much, now did it?

"So, what are you looking so happy about," he said when Len was near.

"If you must know I just had a quite delicious man in there." He pointed a relaxed wrist toward the steam room.

"Which man, if I may be so bold as to pry?"

"Humm, but you'll force yourself, won't you? To be honest, it was kinda hard to see clearly amongst all the steam, but I can say with a degree of certainty it was that lovely man right over there." He pointed toward the bar. "The one talking with Dimity London. The one you thought was so adorable. Her backup singer isn't it?" There was a strong hint of braggadocio in his telling. "What is she doing here by the way?"

"That man's name is Erik. You're sure that's the one you just tricked with?"

"Not completely. We were all of us playing a game of *Clue* in there. I got someone in the steamroom with a candlestick."

"Well, he claims to be straight."

"Really? Huh. I must admit there was a bunch of men in there all at once, with enough arms and legs intertwined that Hindu's should have worshiped at us. I suppose it could have been some other man's prick I grabbed hold of. But, if he is the one I had, the only thing straight about him is that well proportioned cock I quite happily sucked. It was standing straight up and as hard as Chinese algebra." Len leaned in to JB. "Confidentially, he may be pretty, but he's wood. It was like playing with a window mannequin. A nice enough mannequin, but he's strictly trade."

And determined to stay in his closet it looked like. JB wondered why anyone would even want to be closeted at this late date in the gay rights movement. There really is no real reason for remaining closeted any more. Unless you happened to be a Hollywood leading man. Come on, folks, lets be honest, can any one of you watch a Rock Hudson movie now and not think about him being a big mo?

If it was Erik Len had done in the steamroom maybe the poor snook was clinging to the old bi-sexual dodge. Which JB well knew was simply an excuse some men used until they met the man they finally fell in love with. He had in his travels met more than a few men who claimed to be straight but didn't mind another man sucking them off in a dark alley somewhere. In some convoluted fashion inside their tiny heads they convinced themselves that they weren't gay if they played the suck-ee and not the suck-or. That giant leap of rationalization on their part could make just about anything else seem all right. In other words, a hard dick really knows no sexuality.

Len interrupted JB's thinking. "I know how we could tell if he's a member of the club."

"Why? Do you think he knows the secret handshake?"

"Not unless he's paid his dues. But, we could go in the bar there and see what his reaction to me will be?"

JB gave it a few seconds thought. "You know, Len, that could tell us if it was him or not. Or it could give him a massive heart attack. Gay panic at being outed does not become most men."

"JB, he's a customer in a notorious gay hangout. How closeted can he be? If Liberace can still be claiming to be straight while dying from his..." Len made a set of air quotes with his fingers. "...watermelon diet...then you have to admit that anything is possible."

# XI

When JB and Len came into the bar together Erik first saw them over Dimity's shoulder. His face went pale. The blood literally ran out of those cliff-like cheekbones of his. Then his complexion went from ivory to pure white when they both walked up to where he and Dimity were seated and sat down next to them.

JB had to admit he did feel a little sorry for the guy. He remembered the days before he had come out to the world. Of living with the constant fear that someone might find out his secret. How he'd had to force himself to laugh at homophobic and hurtful jabs from insensitive jerkass colleagues. He remembered the pain of having to hear his life and desires described as sick and depraved from Sunday pulpits and conservative demagogues. JB knew that deep down living in the closet was in reality all fart noises and broomsticks. Meaning it was smelly and the place where sad will go to hang itself.

JB took the tact of greeting Dimity as if he was renewing an old acquaintance. He made it all hale and hardy. Good lady met. He also watched for Erik's reaction to Len's presence next to him. What fear Erik had to be feeling right then. The man didn't know if Len was going to say anything or not. His face said a major stroke could be in his immediate future.

Dimity, who was unaware of any undercurrents there might have been floating around, picked up the conversation she and JB had been having from before. She was jabbering away at him as if they were old buddies.

Len, next to JB at the bar, simply nodded in Erik's direction while mouthing the words, "I know you...," then twirled an accusatory finger at him. He grinned and put a fist under his chin to balance his elbow on the edge of the bar while fluttering his lashes at Eric several times. Then he finished up by gracing him with one of his more sly and salacious grins. In essence he was daring Erik to say something. Come on, just admit it why don't you?

It was a situation fraught with the malicious sort of humor that Len so enjoyed. And it was causing some damned uncomfortable squirming for Erik.

JB decided to take a modicum of pity on the guy. He leaned back and said to Len, "I know you're trying for the Prince of Evil here, but its really coming off more like the Lord of Lechery. You can be such a bitch sometimes."

"Really? That's what you think? I'm not trying to be bitchy, JB."

"Hey, you know what? You could use that as the title of that book you've been offered."

So what did Len's latest victim do next?

What he did was grab onto the bar to keep himself steady and standing up while simultaneously trying not to panic—or at the least not show any of the same to anybody else. It was similar to asking an earthquake not to shake a trailer park.

JB could almost see the wheels grinding and meshing together inside his head as he looked for a way out of his situation. How could he explain it? The man who had just seen him doing whatever it was he was doing in a gay steamroom turned out to be acquainted with the lady he worked for. Oy vey!

Like a heifer standing in a herd of sheep Erik realized he was going to find it difficult to hide himself. Any inclinations he might have wanted kept hidden were going to be exposed. Right here. Right now. What to do?

His fist softly hit the leather covered edge of the bar. His face became determined. Not if I can stop it from happening, it said. Not if I can come up with a way out of this mess. Now how would he do that then?

He took a stab at covering his discomfort by flashing his pearly whites at everyone. That smile had gotten him through plenty of bad situations. Like that drug mess last year for instance. A large amount of cocaine in his pockets and Dimity had found him with it. She was still holding that over him like a hangman's noose. As his defense he'd had only his smile, his fear of spending time in prison, and his willingness to do whatever Dimity demanded to save himself from the situation. His asking how high he should jump was what was keeping the bitch from carrying out her threats to ruin him.

This time, however, he could see flashing a smile wasn't going to cut it. The reaction to his grin from JB and Len was stony looks and an awful silence that hung like swamp moss as they waited for him to respond to their implied threat. Beads of sweat broke out on his forehead. He wiped his hands on the towel wrapped around him, and was relieved when Dimity, still blissfully unaware of anything going on among them, yammered on. Erik focused on what she was saying. It didn't even matter what was being said.

She was chattering on, filling in the silence. JB was nodding. Trying to stay interested enough to look like he was listening to her when in reality his attention was focused on Erik. And Len, evil queen that he was, was still sitting there on his perch, vulture like, grinning that most rascally grin

Erik reached over the bar and grabbed part of a stack of cocktail napkins to swipe at his clammy forehead. He ended up holding a wet ball of tissue in his hand. Soggy origami. He looked around frantically for someplace to dispose of it. There was none. This was getting worse for him by the moment.

Len, still perching, had, so far, managed to keep from laughing at Erik's discomfiture. JB, for his part, kept one eye on Erik and one on Dimity, who was still completely oblivious to Erik's predicament.

Erik finally just left the ball of sweaty tissues on the bar and pointedly turned his back to Len. He interrupted Dimity, "I have to leave, honey. But I'm so glad we had this talk. I really do need to get on home."

Erik had decided to deal with his problem by not dealing with it. Typical hetero behavior, JB said to himself. After all, it was the heteros who invented the closet to begin with, wasn't it? There is no sane gay person who would create such a torture device for themselves. So, of course, any straight man would want gays to stay hidden away inside the damned thing. To accomplish that Erik had decided that running away was going to be his choice of action.

At this point JB and Len were thoroughly enjoying the sight of Erik's discomfort. They weren't going to let him get away with simply running and pulling the door to his closet shut behind him. So Len put a stop to Erik's thinking any escape was a viable notion.

"I don't think you'll be going anywhere," he said. "The detective over there has locked this place down tight. No one leaves or enters without his permission. So you'll have to stay whether you want to or not."

"Oh, damn..." Gears in Erik's head came clanging to a stop as he was forced to instantly rethink his exit strategy. "...I-I guess I'll have another drink then."

He stood, picked up a glass, and went off toward Brian the bartender who was standing talking to another customer at the other end of the bar. Putting some distance between him and his embarrassment seemed to be his fall back position.

JB watched him leave, then turned to look at

Len, who just shrugged. What was he supposed to do? He played his cat trapping mouse game enough for the night. There would be little joy in torturing Erik more. "I guess we can deal with him and his, ahem, issues later, right?"

JB nodded, then added "He not going any where any time soon, so we'll know where to find him." He turned back to Dimity. "And you are stuck here as well. Which will give us a chance to talk some more, yes?"

Her armadillo shell was back in place. "Sure, bub. Whatta' ya' got in mind?"

# XII

What Len hadn't considered in his hurry to torment Erik was that by being at the bar it would put him in the direct orbit of Brian the bartender. The one person he really wanted to avoid tonight. Brian was the old acquaintance who wanted to "talk" with him. The man Len had hurt and cheated all those years before. Where exactly any conversation they might have would go he wasn't sure. Len knew he had to make his amends to the man. He had to apologize for his actions back then. He had to try to explain how he had harmed a perfectly innocent person. Would Brian accept his apology? Or would he punch him in the face?

There was history between them, of course. Many years before they had both been struggling actors up for the same part. With the same agent representing them. It was a star part in a brand new soap opera for one of the networks. A prime gig. A star making part. Len had been picked to play the lead over Brian. And Brian hadn't been happy about it. It turned out to be the part that had made Len's career. His part as

Lord Hawthorne in that soap had made it possible for him to become a working participant in the notoriously difficult business of acting.

And poor Brian was now working in the tubs, in lowered circumstances it looked like. Was that what he wanted to discuss with Len? Was there a grudge being held? Did Brian want to confront Len with how his own career had tanked? How Len had ruined his one chance at success? Had Len destroyed his life?

Jeez, Len didn't want to hear any of that. He decided he really needed to absent himself from the situation. Get the hell out of Dodge. He checked on JB, who was still busily engaged in conversation with Dimity. All Len had to do was put a foot on the floor and slowly rise from his stool...

To come eye to eye with Brian standing across from him. Len sat back down.

Brian said, "I'm glad we have this chance to talk, Len..."

Well, running wasn't going to be an option then. Len girded a loin for the tirade to come.

Brian continued, "...I just wanted to say it's all good, man. You and me. We're cool, Len. I don't hold any kind of grudge about the past. I let it go so I could move on. I even spoke to Maxine about it. We're cool too." He smiled and held out his hand for Len to shake.

In a daze Len shook the proffered hand. Brian went on, "It just wasn't meant to happen, Len. That's the breaks of show business. Hey, you did way more with that part than I ever could have. I get why they gave you the part. You were the better actor, that's all. But, I did get to audition for the thing. Seven times."

"I auditioned nine times before I got it," Len said. But his head was shouting back at him—he's letting you off the hook. Let him, Len. You're free. No guilt. Terrific.

But there was another voice inside there steadily getting louder. This one was yelling—but that's not what really happened. Tell him the truth!

# XIII

s JB was about to ask Dimity his first question there came a soft popping sound from outside the bar area. It was a muffled pouf and a slim echo in the tiled hall, soft enough that most wouldn't even register it, nonetheless it got Dimity's attention. She perked up like a Chihuahua, shaking and straining to hear.

"I know that sound. That was a flash bulb firing. Did any of you see a flash of light? It came from a camera." She stood up. "Someone's taking pictures of us. Unauthorized pictures."

JB dismissed it. "It's probably the cops. I'm sure the forensic guys are here by now."

Dimity wasn't having it. "And why would they be taking pictures of me? No, there's some a-hole in here with a camera. Planning to sell pictures to the tabloids I'll bet. Or maybe he wants pictures of you Len. Or your picture JB. You're a well enough known writer. Good for a line or two in a gossip column."

She pulled her robe tight around her waist, then, without warning she was off running. Heading for the stairway. Her screech this time was, "I know you're here, you low-life paparazzi shithead. Come out you!!!"

She didn't stop when she got to the stairs. She began climbing them.

Len came out of his daze to look at JB. Alarm was distorting his features. "What is that crazy woman up to? She shouldn't go up there."

And Len himself was off, after her, leaving JB sitting alone in the bar.

Len caught up with Dimity on the stairs and grabbed at her arm, stopping her for the moment. Then he shouted, in his best carry to the upper mezzanine theatrically trained voice, "Hey! Guy's. There's a *real* lady in the hallways. Shut your door's, you perverted bathhouse queens."

The echo of slamming doors could be heard throughout the building.

That done, he turned to Dimity, "Just how do you plan on catching this guy in these hallways? He could be in any one of a hundred dark corners."

"But he can't get away with this. This is about my personal privacy. He's intruding on it, the worm."

"I think I have an idea where he might be. How about I escort you directly there? With no wandering into any of the other halls."

Len held on to her arm and steered them to the room where Matty Silverman's body was still lying. Len had guessed that any paparazzo in his right mind would want to have a picture of the dead guy to add a dé rigueur sense of authenticity to his story. Len suspected that was where the photographer would be found.

It also afforded him the chance to put some distance between himself and Brian the bartender. He had to think about what he should do with Brian's claim that he had moved on. Should Len tell him the truth and open up the old wound again? Rip off the scab covering it. Or let the matter lie where it was buried?

Meanwhile, back at the bar, JB zeroed in on the hot-looking detective—or should he call him Liam as he'd requested? No, he decided, using the officer's title of Detective would go a long way toward showing JB's respect for the cop's official position. He wouldn't feel right calling him Liam until they'd had a first date. If there was ever one in the offing.

The detective was still engaged in his interrogation of Henry Lavender. The two were sitting several stools down from where JB was.

Easily, so as not to disturb any rapport that the cop and his interviewee had built up between them, JB rose and went down the bar to where they were sitting. He slid himself in behind the detective to quietly listen in on their conversation

Henry was saying, "Matty was a real piece of work. I swear he could start an argument in an empty room. Prickly, you know? Which means he'd pat you on the shoulder with one hand, while twisting the knife he'd placed in your back with the other. But he loved his clients. He kind of mothered all of us. He would have taken a bullet for any of us..." A light went on. "Hey, you don't suppose he *actually* took a bullet for us?"

"We don't have a motive yet. We're looking for a clue. That's why these questions."

Now the detective changed his line of questioning and went for trying to get at who the dead man was personally. "So, Mr. Silverman...was he a mensch or a monster. Which is it?"

Henry considered a second, then said, "I mean I liked Matty, I did, but I wouldn't trust him with my brother."

"So, he was only a weasel, not a monster?"

"That's it. "

A question popped into JB's head. He knew he would probably learn more if he kept his mouth shut, but that wasn't one of his strong suits. Ever. He couldn't stop himself and asked, "What about Matty's relationship with Dimity London? Was that the same sort of thing as you had with him?"

"Well, not really," Henry answered, trying to be as

cooperative as possible. "They were much closer than he and I...Him and me?...closer than we ever were to each other. They were like a couple of sisters, I guess. He was the older show-biz savvy sister, the Mama Rose of the pair, and Dimity was supposed to be the Baby June character. What Matty forgot was that June finally ran away." He stopped, thinking over what he'd just said. "Maybe I should have said they were more like student and mentor. That's closer to the truth. Dimity would listen to Matty when nobody else could get through to her. Although it could be a struggle to get her to do just about anything."

"That explains the earlier argument myself and the rest of the lobby were witness to."

Detective Liam, at JB's question, had turned in his chair to face him with one of those wondering looks on his face. A "Who the hell is interrupting my interrogation" look. Realizing it was JB he smiled and made an exaggerated ushering in gesture. He turned back to face Henry to ask his own next question. Instead Henry was elaborating on JB's observation.

"What you saw was only a pair of siblings fighting, Sisters argue, right? It happened pretty often actually. Between Matty and her. Between Erik and her too. And with me sometimes. Dimity can be a real drama queen. She would try being a dictator with all of us. Hitler in drag. But it was Erik who got the brunt of it. Why he took it from her none of us could figure out. We decided he must be crazy about her. He'll do anything she wants. Even degrade himself." He paused a second, then said, "You understand, she'd not all bad, there are some things you have to admire about the lady. There's a single-mindedness to her. She is all about her career. But Matty was never a pushover for her. Not like Erik. Matty would push back when she tried to lord it over him. Playing Lady Diva. Although, I have to admit this evening's performance was pretty extreme for both of them. Perhaps it was having an audience to watch the hysterics. Show biz types you know?"

※

When Len and Dimity arrived at the room holding Matty's body the coroner's men were zipping him into a body bag, used to provide him some small amount of dignity for his ride out on their wheeled gurney. She lost it for the moment and snuggled onto Len's shoulder to weep. He was standing there naked except for a towel and carefully patting her back to calm her when Len saw the flash of light that Dimity had mentioned seeing before.

Damn, there actually is some photographer loose in the building. "You stay here and I'll be right back. Okay?"

Without waiting for her response he left and headed around the corner to find the photo bomber. What he found was a burned flashbulb from a professional camera lying on the floor. He bent to pick it up. Still warm, it had to have gone off only seconds before. Then he heard a door clicking closed just ahead of where he was bent down.

Len was standing in front of that door in moments. A light knock by him and a tremulous voice inside said, "Yeess?"

Wait a second—Len was struck by a memory dredged from a dark recess of his mind—he knew that voice—He reached for the knob and twisted it.

The door snapped open. Sitting on the cot inside was the person he'd suspected it would be. Benny Foote. Better known as Benny the Brit, because of a thick Cockney accent. Len knew Benny far too well from his own days of being a tabloid target. Benny had taken countless pictures of Len in far too many embarrassing places and positions during his drinking days.

One night, in an attempt to get back the photos he'd taken of a particularly raucous evening at the Oak Room, Len had even taken Benny home for a night of blackmail sex. The experience was, in a single word, grotesque and would certainly never be repeated.

The problem with Benny is that he's—Well—he's short for one thing. Not little person short, just not tall. Perfectly formed and proportioned Benny when standing came up to just above Len's waist. The man would need to bring a stepladder to a glory hole.

There was one other thing to. He was downright creepy. His unsavory profession tended to place him outside the mainstream, on the outer regions of anything near polite society. It left Benny with no social skills to speak of. If you stuck around him for long he came off as an angry little man and a contentious gimp. But tiny. And British. And not your nice cultivated British. Benny was a character written by J.R.R. Tolkien.

Len reached forward and gingerly picked up the camera Benny was holding on his lap. It was one of the old fashioned types, black metal and heavy with a silver flash attachment on the side that resembled a small radar dish. Len clicked the hinge on the rear of the camera and lifted up the now exposed film to the light. "I can't believe you thought you could get away with this, Benny."

Benny yelped, "Hey...What's ya think your doing there, you wanker? That's me own private property."

"Not anymore it isn't. Since the subjects would strenuously object to any use of it."

"Come on, don't be a total git. I'm just trying to do me job."

"It's just a shame your job is picking at people's bones like a pig snuffing out a truffle." Len handed back the now empty camera.

Benny looked crestfallen. "It ain't fair. This was to be a real tickity-boo of a story it was. The headline was to read..." He held his hand up in front of himself, as if scanning a marquee. "FAMOUS AGENT MURDERED IN BATHHOUSE BLOODBATH, under me own personal byline."

"Well, now it going to be in the back of section two..." Len repeated Benny's hand motion. "...UNKNOWN BODY FOUND IN BATHS...without any illustrations." Len turned to leave.

"I still have the test Polaroid's, you know." Benny smirked at his putting one over, then realized he'd opened his mouth a little too soon. Not the sharpest pencil in the box our Benny.

Len turned back and held out his palm. "Okay, let's see em." He wiggled his fingers. Benny reached into his bag and took out a stack of pictures which he reluctantly handed over to Len.

"So what weirdness do we have here?"

Len quickly rifled through the pictures and found several shots of the dead man, including some close-ups that were gross and in questionable taste at best. But none of them were of Dimity or him. Len handed them back. "My, you are a queer little duck, aren't you? And, just so you know, that's an opinion not any sort of gay slur."

# XIV

With the cops and the forensics people packed up and the coroner's guys moving Matty Silverman's body to the morgue the baths quickly returned to the tranquil calm of before. Soon the horny roamers were again wandering the halls like a troupe of Romanian gypsies, all of them hoping to find the man of the moment and move in on him.

When Dimity and Len arrived back at the bar from upstairs they found it was closing down. Brian the bartender was busy wiping the oak surface of the bar with a wet towel, while another of the office clerks was counting out the till. It seemed a bit futile since the bar would open again in only two hours for the breakfast and Bloody Mary crowd. What it did mean was the time had to be somewhere around 4AM in the morning.

The two of them walked in to find Erik and Henry sitting at the bar together, while JB was standing over by the booths talking with another man. That hot cop from before. He stood out here because he was fully dressed. Suit, tie, the works. This was the one who'd left Len to talk with his—who? His work partner? His back-up. His lover? Whatever.

It looked as if the detective was staying around the building to investigate this bathhouse crime further. Len then asked himself if the hunky boyfriend was still stationed in the outside hall? He looked back and saw him by the office window corralling the few stragglers he'd been assigned to watch over.

Dimity peeled off from Len to go sit with her band mates. Len walked over to stand with JB and the cop. The detective was saying to JB. "So, our questioning has let us eliminate at least ninety-five percent of the people here tonight. And strangely enough they all seem to have disappeared from the premises right after we talked to them." He snorted. "We've been left with about six people who have motive enough to have done it."

JB answered, "You need to include the members of Dimity's band that are still here. That includes both Henry and Erik over there. Plus Dimity. All three of them knew the murdered man. Did you know that more than eighty percent of murders are committed by people who know the murder victim."

The detective grinned. JB was instantly smitten with that smile of his. Visions of winged birds ran through his mind as the tune of The Carpenters "Close To You" ran in the background. He shook himself. Get a grip, he told himself.

"You are a smart one, aren't you?" Liam joked.

"That is what it always used to say on my school report cards. Although, it was usually followed with the words ass or mouth. I'm sorry. I mean to be helpful. Not intrusive..."

"No, Mr. Bent, it's really okay...as long as what you have is related to the case at hand."

"Please, call me JB. I'd like it very much it if you did." And he giggled.

Len stared at him. JB had actually giggled. Like some pubescent schoolgirl. Len shook his head. Oh, good Lord, here we go again. JB as his usual everyday self could be a bit hard to take at times. There was that know-it-all thing he tended to flaunt at all and sundry.

But when he became in thrall with someone—well, the man could be downright insufferable.

Although, Len did have to admit he couldn't blame JB for being attracted to the young detective. He was exactly JB's type. And there was a huge bonus in that head of red hair he sported. JB always was a sucker for the ginger boys. Even Len had been a redhead when he and JB met. JB was an A number one pumpkin smasher. The man was the answer that the saying was true—Once you go red you'll bed em' till you're dead. Len chuckled to himself

JB was still talking to the cop. "What's missing in all this is a motive. I'd also like to know why Matty Silverman was shot point blank in the face? Aiming at his chest would have been far more efficient...unless there was something more to it than simply eliminating him. You think it was a revenge thing maybe? Getting even for some old slight? That gun blast does seem excessively spiteful, doesn't it? But, what else could it be?" He paused a moment, then went on, not waiting for an answer to his own question. "It could be anything. Any old reason. I think what we need to do is to find out some more about Silverman himself. There's got to be a reasonable reason for his death. We need to figure out what it was."

The detective asked, "How do we go about that?"

"We could talk to Dimity, Henry and Erik all at once? Then we can compare their stories to what they've already said? It's remarkable, but sometimes the pieces of the puzzle come together from all kinds of different directions."

"And aren't you lucky," Len added, the sarcasm dripping off every word. "There they are all come together like an Agatha Christie cozy. All waiting for Miss Marple to expose the killer. But, where, oh where, is the vicar?"

"Probably dipping into the sherry, the old sot." JB added to go along with the bit.

The detective, less tolerant of Len's theatrics than JB was already walking toward the group of three at the end of the bar. "Are you coming, JB?"

JB smiled at Len. "I'd better catch up. You okay?"

"Fine. I'm just going to sit over here." He pointed to one of the booths.

But Len had to admit that fine wasn't the real truth about how he was feeling. Boy, he chided himself, this honesty thing that AA asks of you could be a real trap. Without the distraction of conversation between the detective and JB Len's mind kept going back to his problem with Brian the bartender. Len just wished his head would stop kvetching at him about it. What was he supposed to tell the guy? How could he explain what had really happened with those auditions?

Brian wasn't there in the bar anymore. He had piled the empty stools up on the bar so the place could be swept, and had gone off somewhere, presumably to find a broom.

So what was Len to do? Should he withhold the truth from Brian, thereby keeping the peace, or should he tell him the real facts about that audition. An audition that took place almost seven years ago, mind you. It isn't as if it's some recent event. Len considered that he wasn't the same person he was seven years ago. Not by a long shot.

He took a mental sigh of resignation as his mind took another leap. It's because I'm not that same person that I have to tell Brian. I need to rid myself of this huge regret for one thing. I'm supposed to be living a life of rigorous honesty in AA. And for better or worse what those people in AA have is what I want. I want the seeming peace and the serenity that comes from being in the fellowship. He decided that he did need to be truthful with Brian. It was as simple as that.

Len's head then snapped to one more possibility. It just isn't all that simple is it? Not really. God—or as the program would have it, his Higher Power—well, that guy has been known to hold an old testament grudge or two, and Lord knows I've done some awful things in this life. Things I shouldn't be forgiven for.

And that's a problem why? Because Len was perfectly aware that no sin ever goes unpunished does it? That's what the whole concept of Karma is all about, isn't it? It's those unchangeable events of your past that haunt you and keep you up at night. And those thoughts will always take you to a drink just to dull the nagging in your head. Listen to it and there you are again, right back where you started. Glass in hand. Your disease holding you in its icy grip again. Len felt himself shutter at the thought of that.

He made up his mind. He would have to make his amends to Brian and beg for his forgiveness. But oh, what a tangle of worms this would open up. If one of the people he'd hurt back in the day gets an apology then they all have to get an apology.

# XV

The three, Dimity, Erik, and Henry, looked to JB with perplexed looks on their faces. Detective Kelly had marched up and without preamble had asked them for their stories. As a result he hadn't been as clear as he thought he'd been. What stories, they wanted to know? Was he expecting "Goodnight Moon" or something? He'd ended up with a confused group of suspects.

"What the detective is saying," JB explained, "is that we've come to the conclusion that this wasn't a random killing. There's is some purpose behind Matty Silverman's death. We're asking you three...who were all intimates of his...if there had been any interruptions to his routine in the last few weeks? Was he acting differently maybe?"

Dimity spoke first. No surprise in that. She was the pushy one of the group. "What are you intimating here?" Suspicion was raising her hackle's again. "Is there something screwy about his death? Do you suspect someone? Not one of us, surely? You can't mean me?" Leave it to her gigantic ego that even another man's death would be turned around to how it affects her.

JB went instantly into conciliation mode. "No one at all. We're merely looking for a motive. A reason for someone to want him dead."

"How about money? Two hundred thousand dollars worth?" Dimity squared the overly padded shoulders of her robe. That brazen hussy act was back in place. "Matty took out an insurance policy. I know about it because I was the witness to it being signed and notarized. Whoever benefits from that policy is gonna be your killer." It seemed plain enough to her, why not to everyone else?

Detective Kelly asked, "When was this? When did you see this policy?"

"It was a couple of weeks ago. He took it out to protect Gunnar. That's his partner..."

JB commented, "Two hundred thousand dollars? That's a lot of protection for anybody. My insurance company is so cheap that to get that kind of money out of them I'd have to die like eight times."

Dimity was warming to her subject. She had begun to sound like a TV talk show host. Merv dishing with the girls. "I know for a fact that Matty had some trouble with the immigration people when Gunnar...that's his boyfriend like I said before...when they first moved here. The INS has trouble believing that gay people love each other the same way straight people do. Matty met Gunnar when he was in Sweden as a cultural attaché with a dance company. They had trouble with the government over green cards and work permits. That sort of thing."

Henry said, "Is that why Gunnar was always cast in Matty's projects? So he'd get to keep his work permit?" He then explained to JB and the detective. "Gunnar was always involved in any of Matty's projects. In some capacity. Stage Manager. Prompter. Assistant to. If you asked Gunnar about it he'd always say that he got his job because he screwed Matty Silverman. Many gay men in New York have foreign lovers. It's a cosmopolitan city after all. And many of them have trouble staying together. The State Department is a very homophobic government agency. But, Gunnar and Matty, well, they've been together for some time so they must have worked it out."

Dimity picked up the ball. She could have put Rona Barrett to shame in the dish the dirt department. "They've been together for years. But they both realized that if anything should happen to Matty then Gunnar would be left out in the cold. One adopting the other was out of the question...there were family objections I guess...so Matty settled on an insurance policy that would take care of Gunnar if he was gone. Is that enough of a reason for him being murdered?"

JB asked the detective. "Is this Gunnar one of your suspects?"

He shook his head. "I just heard the name for the first time right now. He isn't even here tonight. How would he have accomplished it? Unless...he could have hired someone? A hit man? Was it a murder for hire?"

Erik, who had been silent so far, finally spoke up. "That's very unlikely. My uncle is confined to a bed at St. Anthony's Hospital. With some cat disease. Toxioplasmosis, I think its called. Something like that. It's affected his brain. He's really sick."

JB knew of it. One of the downsides of having a suppressed immune system from AIDS was it left you vulnerable to any stray disease hanging around inside your body. Cat diseases, allergies gone mad, thrush. JB had seen men actually bedridden from athlete's foot run rampant. Yeast infections were common. Kaposi's sarcoma was rare until AIDS came along.

"I'm sorry he's so ill." He turned to the detective. "It would make it hard for him to kill someone."

"Like I said. He hired someone."

The uniformed sergeant knocked at the door to the bar. "Sorry to interrupt you, Detective Kelly, sir. The precinct sent these over. I assumed you'd want them right away." He held out a set of portfolio files.

Len, who had wandered over to stand at the edge of the group, took note of the sergeant exhibiting a fair bit of queen like attitude toward his boyfriend/

detective/superior. He was being so formal it hurt. It was plain there was some trouble brewing between the pair.

The Detective noted it also but choose to ignore his partners surly attitude. He waved him in, obviously deciding on a similarly formal response to his presence. "Good. I was waiting for these." He took the folders and laid them down on the bar. Then he spread them out like a riverboat gambler. "These are the arrest records and files of the people still here right now. The ones that might be my suspects. At least the ones that have records with us."

He turned back around. The sergeant was still standing behind him. Waiting. "That's all. You can go back to your post," he said sharply.

The sergeant's face looked startled by the order, or was it more the detective's dismissive tone that he was reacting too?

"But, Liam," he sputtered. "I-I was supposed to..."

The detective reached out, grabbed the sergeant by the shoulder, and pushed him over to the door, while whispering at him, "We'll talk later, Roger. Okay? Right now do as I say." He gave him an entreating look to cap off his plea.

The officer nodded brusquely, turned, and headed for the lobby.

Len was thinking, as he watched this scenario play out, now there's a detective who probably won't get laid tonight.

The detective returned to the group at the bar and said, as an unnecessary explanation, "He's aiming to make detective himself. I said I'd help him, but now isn't the time for that, is it?" While he was offering this he began to run his hands over the folders he had received. Then he flipped the covers open. Paper clipped to the inside of each file was a photo of the offender named.

Len, like each of the other people at the bar was taking surreptitious glances at each of the folders. Seeing if any of them were being implicated in the detective's murder investigation.

They all were. Even Len and JB. Len had a folder because of an incident of public urination into the Plaza fountain one night back during his drinking days and JB got one for his presence at a gay rights rally a few years before. Also included were both Henry and Erik. And even Dimity. They each had only minor offences like jaywalking. Then Len spotted one person in the bunch who was wanted by Interpol, the international police organization. And, as fate would have it—or is that Murphy's Law?—he knew exactly where that man was.

# XVI

When Len had recognized the man pictured in the detective's line-up of suspects he decided, for once, to keep the knowledge to himself rather than blurting it out to everyone present. Instead he began to roll his eyes and dart his head until he finally managed to get Dimity's attention. Then using a few more facial tics, he directed her to take a look at the folder he'd just looked at. She did so.

Her eyes got wide and she looked back at Len with alarm.

He jerked his head for her to meet him outside the bar.

She mouthed an "okay," then stepped over to the detective, interrupting him to say she was going to her dressing room to change out of her robe. He gave her his permission.

She surreptitiously gave a nod to Len as she passed by him on the way to her dressing room at the end of the bar. He then backed out of the bar as quietly as he could to go and wait for Dimity by the palm at the service window. He felt like a character out of a John LeCarré spy novel, or that German acting comic behind a rubber plant on *Laugh-In*.

Standing at the office window, Len was able to hear from inside a snatch of a conversation.

Having hung around with JB enough to accept his theory that an overheard conversation was completely free of copyright, Len stepped in a bit closer to hear better what was being said. He was thinking as a reasonable excuse, if anybody should ask, that the voice might be from a TV and he'd wondered what program was currently playing.

It turned out it wasn't the TV he'd heard, but it could have been a segment from any one of the multitudes of talk shows currently on TV. Sally Jessie, Merv, Tammy Faye. This one was one of those weepy clinging wives segments so popular with afternoon audiences.

The speaker Len had heard turned out to be Roger, the uniformed sergeant/boyfriend, talking into his walkie-talkie. The voice coming back to him, even in the garbled state Len was able to hear, was certainly that of Detective Kelly. Len swung around to take a look back into the bar. Sure enough, the detective was standing away from the others and talking into his own walkie.

Turning back to the window, Len picked up a copy from the stack of the latest issue of the *New York Native* stored there. He pretended to be interested in an ad for the latest gay cruise to Jamaica. What fun that must be? Stuck on a ship with a thousand bitchy queens all looking to get laid by a stray Rastafarian— What he was really doing was listening in on the single side of a conversation. A conversation that tended to fade in and out as the sergeant paced back and forth across the outer window.

What Len got was, "But, Lee, I didn't mean..." Thus verifying that the voice on the other end was indeed the detective's. Also it meant that the two men were close enough for the cop to call his boss by a nickname.

"Well, I am angry with you. Can you blame..." And there was the guarantee that the two men were having some sort of affair. Which seemed to be going through a rocky patch at the moment.

The sergeant finally stopped his pacing to stand in front of the outer window. Len became interested in an ad for a computer dating service. 1-800-HOT-GUYS. At $3.00 a minute! It would be way cheaper for the caller to be paired with a couch, a bottle of hand lotion, and some porn.

"Lee," the Sergeant was saying, "I saw you eyeing that writer guy. What's up with that? Are you dumping me for that old queen? You can't be..."

At hearing this Len's mind went completely on to another track—What! his head was shouting at him, Wait a second? Could the old queen the sergeant was talking about be JB? His friend JB? Good God, we're the same age! And this rude punk-ass twink thinks JB is old! That's not possible. And very tactless of the little whippersnapper. But then how old does a person have to be to actually use the word whippersnapper?"

"Can I get to the window, Len?"

Len started and stepped back. "Crips, JB, you scared the hell out of me. You shouldn't creep up on people like that."

"I don't creep. I arrive stealthily." JB stepped past Len and stood at the window. "So why are you here?"

Len searched quickly for an answer. "Oh, I was going to ask to get the dead man's things. I thought the detective might want them."

"Wow," JB exclaimed incredulously. "I don't believe it. You've had exactly the same idea I did? What made you think of getting Matty's envelope of personal items? The detective only just said that it was a good idea, and sent me out here for them."

"Well, there you go underestimating me again, JB. I could be a PI just as well as you, you know? You aren't the only person who thinks logically around here tonight. And I bet I could turn right around and write about it too."

JB's eyebrows rose on his forehead. "I'm sure you could." He leaned into the window and spoke to the clerk while wondering what it was that had gotten up Len's craw all of a sudden? He wasn't usually this defensive. It must be one more manifestation of his newly found sobriety. It was, after all, only a few months since he started down this new path of his.

JB knew, from attending a few Al-anon meetings, of several people who went through complete personality changes when they started living sober. Partnerships of long standing would suddenly fall asunder. Straight men would realize they were gay. Friends would stop being friends. Many gay men would suddenly chafe at the old, now thought to be stale, relationships they were in. The trips these men took to a non-drinking existence could play hell with someone's idea of who and what they were all about. Fun guys changed to judgmental pricks. Bitches became Pollyanna's. And it was never only the sober guy going through it. All of his acquaintances got to go along for the ride too. Or they often wouldn't stay friends. Was his friend now going to become a different person?

He turned back to face Len. "I think it's really cute that you think so much of yourself, sweetie. But you know that the person you're so in love with can be a royal pain in the ass sometimes." The clerk handed over the envelope of Matty Silverman's processions. "Now, do you want to see what's in here?"

Len's attention, in just those few seconds, had been drawn elsewhere. He waved JB off. "I'll be along in a minute. There's something I need to do first."

# XVII

hat had grabbed Len's attention was the bank of small TV monitors lined inside the bathhouse office. They monitored the security cameras that were placed strategically around the building. From what Len could observe they covered the ground floor but not the hallways upstairs. That would mean there wasn't any video of the person who had gone into Matty Silverman's cubical and shot him. That was a bit of bad luck.

But what was keeping Len's interest right then was the picture on one of the monitors. The screen was taking pictures of the outside basketball court. Located at the end of the hall directly down from the office, the courts weren't used all that often for playing games, but was the site of the building's *Cinco de Gayo* celebration and BBQ in the spring.

Right that moment it was being used as the parking spot for a beat-up Volkswagen inside the wire mesh fencing that separated the courts from the street. And who should be opening the door of that VW but none other than Benny the Brit, wanted by both Len and it turns out—Interpol.

Dimity chose that moment to come up beside Len. She asked what he was doing. He turned and saw that she had changed into one of those awful velour jumpsuits that were so popular with Staten Island housewives. Hers was a bilious violet with rhinestones scattered over it like bird droppings. There were also different shades of purple leather making a mosaic that covered the front, went  over the padded shoulders, and trailed down the back. Tacky. Tacky. Tacky. Len stepped back and took an appraising look. Really, ample sized people shouldn't wear leather, he was thinking. If you're shaped like a football you shouldn't dress like one. "Egad," he said. "What the hell are you wearing?"

She looked down, then back at Len. "What? I went for comfort. So, you're such a fashion maven now?"

"I'm gay, so of course I am. I just thought you might have gone a bit subtler because of your friend Matty being gone. You're not grieving I take it."

"I have on black underwear. So there." She held up a single finger.

"Fine. So take a look at that." He pointed to the monitor. "It would seem our Benny is trying to make a fast exit."

Dimity looked at the monitor and grabbed Len by the arm to shake him, saying loudly, "We've got to stop him."

She started to run down the hall toward the outside door—well, actually it looked to Len more like a lope. If she had been shod there was a chance she could have won the trifecta out at Aqueduct—At any rate, there were heavy feet stomping toward the back door. Len leaned in to tell the clerk that the alarm was going to go off, and then took off after her.

The wail from a siren blared for a moment as Dimity hit the door and pushed it open. Len followed to stand outside and watch her attack the car. Literally.

She jumped every pound of her hefty self on to the hood as if she was an Italian widow falling on a coffin. The car's springs groaned in response. She started slapping at the window to get Benny's attention. This was a pretty effective measure, at first. But being such a big girl, Dimity couldn't maintain her—you should excuse the expression—seat on the hood of the car. She began to slide backward. She ended up leaning over the hood with her hands out wide to prevent Benny from driving away. It was excessive on her part, since the car's motor wasn't even running.

Taking into consideration he was barefoot Len picked his way carefully across the graveled tarmac toward the side door of the VW. As he did he knew he must resemble nothing less than some dainty winged fairy stepping on rocks across a running brook? Like that *White Rock* sprite. Len then wondered if that was a gay slur too?

Good God, he realized, his mind could make the most enormous leaps in seconds, couldn't it? An intellectual Superhero he was—able to leap tall... Well, stop it, he admonished himself. You should leap back to the event at hand.

When he got to the car door he leaned down to look into the side window. He knocked on the glass. Benny rolled down the window and tried, with little success, to look as innocent as a nun on Sunday.

Len asked, "Just where do you think you're going, mister?" He wondered if Benny had to sit on a stack of phone books to reach the wheel of the car? Were there blocks on the pedals?

"Uh, nowhere mate," Benny answered, showing crooked and stained teeth in a cringe worthy smile. "Only bringin' out some things to hide away in the boot." Just then the CB radio on the VW's dashboard crackled as a police call announced a B&E on the Upper East Side at 75th and Park. Benny quickly leaned over and flipped the monitor off.

"So that's how you manage to track people down? I always wondered how you could be everywhere."

"No big trick, me old sod." He chuckled.

Dimity, by then, had taken it upon herself to open the hood of the car. She was leaning in to look over the contents of Benny's trunk. "You have to see this, Len. It's unbelievable," she shouted.

Len asked, "What have you got in there, Benny?"

Benny shrugged. "Just a bunch of old codswallow. Nothing of importance."

Len wasn't having it. "Come on, out of the car." Len opened the door. What do you know? He did sit on a padded romper seat—Benny slid out and slithered over to where Dimity was standing. He seemed almost as curious as Len was.

What Dimity had done was tear open a large black plastic bag she'd found among the other debris packed in the trunk. She held up a sheaf of papers and envelopes. "It's garbage, Len. He's taken people's garbage right out of their cans." She held out a few envelopes. "These all belong to Calvin Kline."

"Not everything a bloke throws out is garbage you know. You'd be amazed how much you can find out about a person from their pitch outs." Benny chuckled, which reminded Len of Igor in the Frankenstein movies.

"And look there, he's got files on people." She was pointing at a cardboard box stuffed with manila folders. Len leaned in to start flipping through them.

"Christ, there's a file on all of us," he said. "You. Me..." Len stood up straight holding a folder. "And this one is on Matty." He looked at Benny. "This is stalker material, my friend. Or should I call you Alistair? Since that's your real name." Alistair Foote had turned out to be Benny's birth name according to the Interpol file Len had seen. "Where did the name Benny come from then? That's right, bucko, I know who you really are. And wanted by Interpol at that? What are you? Some sort of international spy or something?" Len snorted. "Although you certainly don't look anything like a James Bond."

"What am I supposed to look like, mate? All cloak and daggerish? No, MI6 isn't interested in me. Not anymore, anyway. Back in England I was a legit journalist, I was. Worked with *The London Morning Sun*. But I needed to fit in over here. Alistair wouldn't have fit in with the blokes I run with here. Far too prissy a moniker for a nightcrawler. So I changed it. Is that against the bloody law."

Not against the law, no, but Len suspected that there might be more to the name change than Benny was letting on. Alistair as a moniker might have been more than our Benny was able to live up to. A way to posh sounding name for the character Benny turned out to be. His parents must have had very high hopes for their little boy. But that wasn't how it worked out. The same way Archie Leach became Cary Grant or Leonard Sly became Roy Rogers to better fit their personas, our Benny had lost Alistair to wallow in his own special sewer as Benny. Going so far as to muck around in the shabby world of the tabloids.

Len said, "You worked at *The Sun* did you? That's one of the worst of the British tabloids, isn't it? So you didn't wander far from your mother's teat when you came over here to America. But, I must say, rummaging around in someone's trash is going pretty far, don't ya think, Alistair? You could actually be arrested for this."

"For what? Garbage collection? Once it's on the streets it's in the public domain. It's not the first time I've collected this sort of thing either. It's quite normal where I come from. I even done it to Mrs. Thatcher, I did. Got into her home office waste bins once. Found a real trove of good gossip. I got three bylines out of that haul, I did."

"Is that why Interpol is looking for you? Did you stumble onto some state secret or something?"

"Well, it weren't the Profumo Affair mind you, but it were juicy what I found. I found meself in a run around with the Royals." Benny leaned in and lowered his voice conspiratorially. "Everybody in England knows that Prince Charley has been fooling around on his Mrs...Princess Di...with another bird." He winked. The gesture seemed to Len somehow dirty. He tried to avoid shuttering.

Benny went on. "I found out who the other woman was. I had the proof right there in me hands. But the palace wouldn't have it surfacing. They managed to squash what I had and me career at the same time. That's why Alistair Foote left home and came across the pond to become Benny."

"Looking for fresh scum, no doubt?"

Benny looked around as if a sniper were zeroing in on him. "Princess Di calls that other woman The Rottweiler. Hates her she does. Believe me, it's going to get real messy if it ever gets out."

"And you'll be there slobbering all over it I bet. I have a dog at home that I'm quite sure you're related to."

# XVIII

itting at the bar JB opened up the bathhouse security envelope and tipped out the contents. The remains of Matty Silverman. A brown zippered leather portfolio plopped undramatically onto the waxed wood. Smaller than a briefcase it was stamped in gold with Matty's initials by the leather handle.

"That's his day planner. He always carried it," Henry said.

JB unzipped it and laid it open. Inside were not only the pages of his appointment book, but also his checkbook, a plastic holder with a Visa and a Diners Club card, along with a plastic holder for his Walkman tapes. He was into *Genesis* and *Wham!*.

"It looks more like he kept his whole life stored in this thing." The thought ran through JB's head that wasn't it sad that this man's life was complete in such a tiny briefcase. He ran his finger down the list of appointments Matty had kept during his last week.

"Humm, he was a busy boy. Let's see, he had a doctor's appointment yesterday. With a Dr. Blickley."

JB looked at the three others gathered along the bar. "You know anything about that?"

Erik said, "That's the name of my Uncle Gunnar's doctor. He's very popular with the queer crowd here in Manhattan."

Henry added, "What makes him so popular is he's one of the few doctors around that treats his gay patients with some respect and decency. There's never any condemnation from him. Most doctor's have a real nasty attitude about people with AIDS, but Dr. Blickley doesn't."

JB knew what Erik was referring to. He had read several articles in the New York papers about the problem. It had been reported that so called medical professionals, who were supposed to live by an oath to aid and care for the sick, were reluctant to deal with the growing number of AIDS patients that were flooding the medical system. These nurses and doctors would isolate and ostracize these poor sick men, not treating them with even the slightest degree of concern or dignity. Nurse's aides would put dinner trays outside the doors of their patient's rooms rather than go inside with them. If you wanted to visit a friend it meant you would have to wear a gown, a mask, and even latex gloves before you were allowed into their rooms. It was all unneeded and despicable treatment. And it didn't help that *The* New York *Native,* a gay paper at that, would splash the most ridiculous claims across their front pages every week. In tabloid style these articles would blame every whack-a-doo theory some barely accredited professional would come up with for the origin of the disease. One week it was green monkeys, another week it was swine flu. Or it was some kind of sinister plot by the CIA to wipe all the gay people off the face of the earth—that theory stopped working when straight men were being diagnosed at the same rate as gay men.

"Why was Silverman seeing a doctor who specializes in AIDS patients?"

"Maybe he was there about Uncle Gunnar? He's very sick. That cat disease thing he has is making him lose touch with reality completely. He's close to total dementia now. Last month, before he was hospitalized, he set fire to Matty's apartment door. He used a can of lighter fluid and turned it into a bonfire."

JB, still looking at Matty's book, had moved on to his checkbook. He checked the balance. "Not an outrageous amount. Only a couple of hundred dollars. Where did he keep his real money?" He looked at Henry.

"It's probably on deposit in a separate account. That checkbook you have there would be only for his miscellaneous expense account. Carrying around money for Matty."

"How do you know that?"

"I already told the Detective. Matty wasn't only Dimity's manager. He was mine too. I write music. Mostly it's been commercial jingles so far. But I won't do that forever. I have all the songs written that I need for an album. And I have a musical for Broadway I've been working on. You see, the problem was Matty was making a healthy commission off all my agency work. He didn't want me to stop doing it. I recently decided to leave Matty's management, but he wasn't having it. He threatened to file an injunction against me. Really, I was trying to keep it all amicable, but Matty could be a real bastard if he was crossed."

JB had been listening to Henry, but was scanning Matty's agenda at the same time. "I don't get it," he said. "There's nothing in his appointments about that insurance thing Dimity mentioned. You'd think it would be listed in here somewhere."

"Maybe it's under the name of his insurance agent," Liam suggested.

Henry agreed. "Matty would always try for a personal touch with the people he met. He always used first names, glad-handed them, patted them on the back... that car salesman sort of thing."

"Then there's no way of finding out about that policy?"

"Maybe I can help?" Dimity said. She and Len —with a very reluctant Benny in tow—had arrived and were standing in the entrance to the bar while JB and Henry were talking.

"Remember JB," she went on. "I was the witness when he got that policy. I was with him when he signed it. I met him at some office over in midtown. After we finished he took me to lunch at *Serendipity.*"

"So the office was on the East Side," JB asked.

"Right, but what the hell was that insurance guy's name?" She thought for a moment. "Oh, I got it. It was Cripliver. Herbert Cripliver." She laughed, except that Dimity's laugh was more of a bray. You hoped it would end soon. "You don't forget a name like that so easily." She thought another moment. "But what the company name was?" Her finger tapped her chin. "No, I don't remember. Sorry."

"Could it be New York Mutual?" Len, who was still standing beside her, with Benny next to him, spoke up. "That's an educated guess you understand." He stepped forward and held up the stack of Polaroid's he'd confiscated from Benny.

JB looked at him. "What's that you have there? Its got to be something good since you have one of the most wicked grins on your face. All you need is a poison apple and a magic mirror."

"Oh, JB, you have no idea what an evil queen I can be."

"I think I do. I've lived with you, remember?"

Len chose to ignore JB's tacky comment for the moment. He would be the better person. This time. Retribution could come later. He held out the photos. "Take a look at those will you? Benny took them before Silverman was taken away." He handed the photos over to the detective.

Liam looked through them one at a time, with JB hovering over the detective's shoulder to get a better look for himself.

Len could taste a little bit of bile rise in his throat as he saw JB actually take a surreptitious whiff of the cop's hair. Oy!

JB smiled. Humm, coconut, his head said, but out loud JB said, "What is it I'm looking for here, Len?"

"Find the close up of the barbell piercing Matty's nipple. That's the one I found the most interesting."

JB separated that picture from the stack.

Len handed over a photographer's loupe he had also taken from Benny. "Do you see the gold markings on the barbell? Look at them with the loupe."

JB remembered that he had said something earlier about the decorative markings on the piece of jewelry Matty was wearing. It now appeared they were there for a reason? JB held the loupe over the picture, squinting to bring the details into focus.

He looked up at Len, then back down at the loupe. "I'll be damned," he said. He looked at Len again, then handed the picture over to the detective.

Repeating JB's action Liam looked at the photo. He said, "Damn. It's the policy number, isn't it?"

Magnified the picture gave clarity to a series of gold filled numbers neatly engraved on the silver ball of Matty's barbell. What JB had initially mistaken for fancy decorative swirls were in actuality letters and numbers. It read, NYM108...

Len said, "What do you want to bet those are the first numbers of that two hundred thousand dollar death policy with his insurance company?"

"You may be right. But this picture doesn't show the whole ball. Some of the numbers aren't visible."

"But the letters are. And I bet you they stand for the insurance company. NYM. Ergo...New York Mutual. You could call them and get the rest of the policy number from them."

"How do you know that?"

"What? It's not enough that I know something, now I have to know how I know something? It's a wild guess, JB."

The detective scratched his head. "I don't understand. Why in hell would he have this information put on a nipple barbell? I would have put it in a safer place myself."

"I agree. How paranoid does one have to be to be that secretive? A desk drawer would have served him just as well?"

Len volunteered his own theory. "Maybe it's the same thing as the sailors that manned the old whaling ships. They wore gold earrings so that if they were washed overboard and their bodies landed on a foreign shore they would have the money for a Christian burial. Engraving it on the barbell at the very least guaranteed that the information would be found."

JB was again looking at Matty's appointment book. "Here it is. Dimity, you were right. The name Cripliver is written in here. At 9 AM." He laid the book back on the bar. "And with the same initials behind it. N-Y-M. So New York Mutual as his insurer does make perfect sense." He said to Liam. "We'll need to call that number when their offices open in the morning."

Liam said. "Maybe not all that long. What time is it anyway?" He checked his watch. It was closing in on 6AM. "I have a friend that works at New York Mutual. On their international desk. He's probably at work this early. Because of the time difference between here and where he does his deals. I'll bet he's at work already. Let me call him."

The detective went off to find a phone.

Len was telling JB that he'd gotten the idea to look at the photo of Matty's nipple under magnification when he'd remembered JB saying the barbell on Matty was so fancy. He'd seen that close up picture of Matty's tit when he'd first confronted Benny in his room. But it hadn't really registered until he'd seen it again when it turned up in Benny's car trunk.

"Well, that was a very nice piece of detective work, Len. Are you trying to give me some competition?"

"I'm helping, JB. Only adding in my two cents. It's up to you to make it into a dollar."

JB looked at him with a narrowed eye. "Do I go on stage every night and say your lines, Len? Do I sing your big eleven o'clock number?"

Len was taken aback. More by the tone than the words. Why was JB getting so territorial all of a sudden? What had brought this bit of bitchery on? "Fine. I'll stay out of it then." Len held up his hands.

He stepped away and went over to sit with Dimity and Henry, who were together at the other end of the bar. As Len sat he said to Henry, "There are rumors that say you're working on a musical? Is that right? You know, I'm currently in a musical?" The actor's hustle had begun.

"I am and I do know."

"Well, don't hold it in, my dear. What's this play of yours all about?"

Henry warmed to Len's question right off. "I'm calling it *The Drag*. It's loosely based on the life of Julian Eltinge. Have you heard of him?"

Len nodded. "I have. He was the teens and twenties female impersonator, right? There was even a theater named after him back in the day. It's now the Empire over on 42nd Street."

"That's the one. There are hints of other drag queens in my show too. Like T.C. Jones and Charles Pierce. I think it could be a smash."

"Hmm. *The Drag*? You know with *La Cage* and the movie *Victor/Victoria* such big hits it does have some possibilities. You've been writing the songs have you?"

"Words and music." Henry was on a roll. "You know, there's this famous picture of Eltinge. It's a trick shot of him in bridal drag marrying himself. So I used that and I've written a duet where the lead sings with himself. Cool idea, huh? The problem I've been having is with the book. I don't have a real story."

"Sings with himself..." Len's ego, always arriving at the corners of Self and Self-centered, was tickled by the notion of a Self-duet. "Maybe I could help you? Could I hear some of the music?"

Excited that a Broadway somebody was interested in his idea, Henry quickly agreed. He led Len right out of the bar and down into the pit where his piano awaited.

# XIX

iam had gone off on his own in search of a telephone. Which he found in the bathhouse office. Once permission was granted by the clerk he first clicked on nine for an outside connection, then, using his own notebook directory, punched in the office number of his insurance friend.

While waiting for him to answer he looked up and realized the mistake he'd made. By using this phone he had exposed himself to being seen from the lobby. Where Roger—who was still assigned to that area—could easily see him.

On one of Rogers passes by the office window he did spot Liam. It then took only a second for him to appear at the window demanding of the startled clerk to allow him in.

Liam's first inclination was to say no when the clerk looked to him for permission. But he had known all along that this confrontation was coming. He decided to get it over with Roger here in a semi-public place. It would, he hoped, be more civilized here rather than waiting until they were alone in his apartment.

This was because waiting until later for the discussion would have made Liam more vulnerable to Roger and his temper, which was not a position he wanted to be in. As Liam had discovered over the past weeks Roger could have violent tendencies. Most of the time he was docile as a bunny rabbit, but only the week before—over some imagined tryst he had accused him of—his tantrum had caused Liam to become fearful for his own well-being. Throwing pieces of furniture against walls was never a good sign in any relationship.

Liam, in his first job on the beat, had been called too far too many instances of domestic abuse between pairs of Upper West Side gay men. It had taught him to be very afraid of the violence that could come from these male on male domestic altercations. The fact that Roger was taller than Liam by several inches, and outweighed him by at least sixty pounds didn't bode well for the situation either. Roger had also taken police hand-to-hand training at the Academy. Liam was well aware all that pointed to a dangerous combination, especially when you further factored in that Liam had the same training and could get his own dander up when the situation called for it. Liam had as high a testosterone level as Roger. Two Alpha males in a household was always a strain. Put those same two males in a sack full of emotional pain and you'd be left with a clusterfuck of epic proportions.

So far, Roger hadn't actually attacked or hurt Liam but those pieces of broken furniture clearly showed the path he was heading down. That, along with some cutting remarks and vicious put-downs from Roger had determined Liam to break off their current arrangement. This just might be the time to do it.

Liam hung up the phone before it could ring through.

As for Roger, he was already pissed when he came in the office, and only just managed to hold his tongue until the clerk—at Liam's suggestion—went out to the bar for a break.

Then Roger yelled. With no escalation, no sliding

up to his anger. It was just there, full out from the start. No preamble, just raw unrestrained fury spewing like bile and aimed directly at Liam. He was yelling with everything he had. "How can you do this to me?" Spittle landed on Liam's face.

So Roger was feeling put upon and disrespected. Never a good thing for a bully to be.

Roger moved in close and began to shake a fist at Liam. "You were everything to me," he said, not even slightly restraining himself. "But I can see it now. I'm nothing to you anymore. I see it in your eyes..."

"You might make detective yet, Roger. But I'll admit I'm kind of afraid of you right now. I hate this violence in you. You have got to get a grip on it, Roger. This kind of uncontrolled anger is nothing to play at. It's definitely the worst of you. You need to talk these things out not just swing wildly at them."

Rogers tone dropped a notch. "Anger you say? Okay, I'll admit to that. I have it in spades" He tapped his chest, reminding Liam of simians at the Bronx zoo. "There's all kinds of anger inside here. Old wounds. New slights. I can't help it...I feel it rising up in me." He racked a hand through his hair. "The heat of it fills me. I feel it in my jaw. In my chest. In my fists." He made one and held it toward Liam. "And it needs somewhere to go or it chews up my gut. I have to get rid of it. So I throw stuff. It helps me to keep my balance. Like a valve. Put it under too much pressure it has to blow. That's when I lash out. I can't stop it. Like...now..." Rogers fist pulled back to hit out blindly.

Liam reached up to grab hold of Rogers fist with his own hand before it could swing. He grabbed hold and braced himself keeping Rogers swing in check. For that moment the two men were two immovable forces holding each other stationary.

Through clenched teeth, Liam threatened him. "Roger, I'm telling you this for your own good. You might hit me this time. Sure. But if you do it will be this one time only. I know you're bigger than me. And you could probably hurt me bad. But I'm warning you. We live together. And you have to go to sleep sometime. That's when I'll stand over you and beat the living hell out of you with a length of rubber hose." He stared straight into Rogers flushed and angry face. Moderating his tone he slowly added, "I will put your ass in traction, motherfucker."

They stood locked in position for a long moment—then Liam finally saw the fire extinguish its self from Rogers eyes. They went blank for a second as Roger took a deep breath and let his fist go down to his side. He got himself back in check.

Liam took a second for his own anger to calm down in a silent sigh, then said to Roger "I want you out of the apartment by Monday morning. Now, get back to your post, Sergeant." He turned his back on his now ex- lover. "I have a phone call to make."

Liam soon returned to the bar and went right over to stand next to JB. Len, watching them from his vantage point at the piano in the pit, couldn't help noticing that they acted like a pair of great old friends. Two attractive men who, even on their short acquaintance of only that evening, had already become intimates. Len had seen this sort of thing happen with JB at least one other time before. JB having that quick intimacy with another man. It had happened between JB and Len only a few years before.

Liam took the stool next to JB and said, "My guy was at work already. He's found Matty's policy, and he's sending over a fax of it to us. It'll be here soon."

JB was now searching through the wallet that he'd found also stored in Matty's envelope. He unzipped it and checked all the slips of paper. He found, along with about fifty dollars in small bills, a prescription from the same doctor that had been mentioned in his date book. The script was for something called Romazeapam.

JB handed the prescription to Liam and asked, "Do you know what that is?"

Liam shook his head. JB rose on his stool and spoke to the people sitting there in the bar. That was Dimity, Erik, Benny, and Brian the bartender. Where were

Henry and Len then? He spotted them seated together at the piano in the pit. What's that about? JB wondered. He'd have to check with Len later, right now there were more important facts to be found out.

He asked loudly, "Has anybody here ever heard of a drug called Romazeapam?"

"Sorry, I don't have a pharmacopoeia handy," Brian the bartender answered rather snarkily, effectively cutting his tip in half.

"It's a drug, right?" That was Dimity.

"I'm not a doctor..." From Erik.

Len having heard JB's voice carry out to the pit shouted back, "Maybe there's a nice hunky looking medical student floating around somewhere in the rest of this place." He smiled. "Would you like me to check?"

And before JB or the detective could voice any objection he abandoned Henry at the piano and climbed the central staircase headed for the rooms upstairs.

JB turned to Liam. "He may be awhile up there. Hunky med students are one of Len's weaknesses. Along with hunky dock workers, hunky professional wrestlers, cooks, busboys...Actually you put anyone hunky in front of Len and he'll go for it. It's a kind of a Pavlovian response on his part."

One of the bathhouse staff stuck his head into the bar area. "There's a fax here for a Detective Kelly. Is that anyone hanging out in here?" Liam stood and walked toward the boy. He knew the kid had the copy of the insurance policy his victim had taken out right before he turned up dead.

Liam was hoping it might hold a piece of information about who his killer might have been. The London woman was probably right when she said whoever got the money was his perp. Always follow the money. That's rule number two in the detective manual, right after the victim knew his killer. This copy of Matty's Silverman's insurance policy might go a long way toward explaining some of the questions that have been surrounding this case. It could also give him a someone to focus on and prove guilty of the crime.

The only recently appointed Detective Kelly could use something to get this case solved quickly. He needed a quick win to impress his Captain back at the precinct. The fact he was among the youngest detectives on the force at twenty-nine hadn't gone very far with the man. It didn't help Liam around the station house much either. His quick rise from the beat into their unit only made him seem precocious—or worse, an overachiever after their jobs—to the cops he worked with. Still, if it could only be as simple as making some quick arrest for his Captain to be the solution to his problems.

What was making the job so difficult was his membership in *GOAL*,—which was an acronym for the New York City Gay Officers Action League. The group had been formed only a scant five years before, so Liam was one of a very small number of out officers on a force that accepted gay cops grudgingly at best.

It had been only a few years before that raiding gay bars was a standard Saturday night event. Pull up the Black Mariah, load it with fags, bust a few heads if they balked, carry them off to the Tombs. The "good old days" as too many on the force still felt it should be.

It was because of his being gay that he was the lone officer assigned to these kinds of cases to begin with. These cases—meaning anything that concerned the queers—was what Liam almost always was compelled to deal with. That was because the rank and file officers in the precinct considered gay cases "soft".

When he'd first arrived it would usually be him alone at a site. Straight cops didn't want to deal with any kind of pervert stuff, so Liam got them all. Before he was promoted to detective he sometimes had to deal with dangerous and violent altercations between a couple of two hundred and fifty pound men with anger issues. After he ended up with a couple of broken ribs his Captain had finally assigned a uniformed officer to partner with him.

The calls they usually went on concerned men who were picked up in a bar then attacked and robbed for being gay. And the bar fights, of course. That raging testosterone thing wasn't only confined to straights.

But having a partner hadn't really helped Liam so much. It had ended up leading to a bigger complication.

Liam and his Sergeant had taken to sleeping together.

The affair, however, wasn't working for Liam. As it turned out, Roger was a hot guy with a mean streak, and Liam had no intention of putting up with that kind of temper from anyone, especially someone he was supposed to love. That's what had led to the uncomfortable scene in the bathhouse office.

And now Liam was handling this murder case. Solving it quickly and cleanly would go a long way toward getting him a bit of respect from the other cops in his precinct. And, though he was loath to admit it, he wanted that. The other men hasn't accepted him. He was barely tolerated by them. Constantly whispered about behind his back, some even went so far as to spew their bigot shit right to his face. Always mumbled at him as he passed by—"pansy" and "fairy" said under their breaths. It happened every day. It was the same sort of name calling school yard bullies indulged in.

His Uncle Collin had advised him to keep his head down and do his job. Assuring him that, eventually, he would be accepted by his coworkers. But it was taking a long time to happen. And it was hard to take. Only the week before someone had scratched the word "faggot" once again on his locker. It cut to the quick. More than he cared to own up to. But he didn't report the incident because it would have made him seem like a whiner. That was a reputation he really didn't need either. So he'd swallowed his pride and let the incident pass.

Liam shuffled the thin fax papers until he found the beneficiary portion of the insurance policy. He wasn't all that surprised to find, as Dimity had said, that one Gunnar Norske got the money. All two hundred thousand of it. What did take him by surprise was a couple of paragraphs down there was a codicil to the policy. It stipulated that if any of the beneficiaries to his estate should question the policy, or in anyway hinder its payout to the beneficiary, then any monies they had been bequeathed in his will would become null and void. In other words, if they protested Gunnar getting the insurance money then they would get nothing for themselves. That was unusual.

"Not if you'd seen the relatives of our dead friends swoop in and take everything from a surviving mate. They'd take everything and leave him with nothing..." It was Henry—he'd returned to the bar after Len went off in search of his hunky med student—responding to Liam's question about the codicil. "...I was pre-law at Columbia before I got into show biz. That addendum would be considered unusual but is perfectly legal. It's unfortunate, but gay men have to go to these sorts of lengths to protect their loved ones. We've all seen it happen to someone we know."

"Great. Now I've got a suspect for the murder. The beneficiary did it."

JB turned to face Liam. "But there's a problem with that idea. Your beneficiary is confined to a hospital bed with a disease that has him acting crazy."

"I don't mean to be all judgey here, but isn't this exactly the sort of thing that a lunatic would do?"

"Detective, the two operative words here are confined and hospital."

"He's right," Dimity said. "How could Gunnar manage something like this...as sick as he is...from a hospital room?"

"Like I said before. This Gunnar guy hired someone to do his dirty work for him."

JB shook his head. It was a problem he had seen over and over with the police. They would focus on one suspect and reject anything that might make their case unstickable. Not actually railroading their perp perhaps, but certainly being narrow and overzealous. "Sorry, but that really seems unlikely given that Gunner is so sick. Ask Erik. He would know if his uncle was capable of something like this."

Liam looked up and down the bar. There was no one except Dimity, JB, and himself anywhere near. Even Henry, who had been there only minutes before was now missing. He asked, "Where the hell is Erik? For that matter where is everyone else?"

"They wandered off while you were discussing things

with JB," Dimity answered. "As for me, I'm confined to the bar here. God forbid I should see some sort of Chinese sex circus going on." She airily waved a hand. "They're all somewhere in the building I suppose"

Liam exploded. "Damn it! I want them all here where I can keep my eye on them. I think this Gunnar guy got himself a hitman to come here tonight and off our victim. And it's one of the people still here in the building. I'd bet my badge on it."

"Then you've got an even bigger problem, Detective," This came from a voice at the doorway. All three faces turned to look at Len standing in the door with one of the T-shirted staff members. He went on. "This place right now is about as popular as New Coke turned out to be. You cops being here have turned this place into a giant parking lot. There's no one in the halls. All the doors are shut tight. The steam room is empty. The orgy room echoes when you walk through it. Any suspects you might have found here tonight have probably already skedaddled. But." He held up a finger dramatically. "I did manage to find you an NYU med student working in the office. He has his PDR with him and he'll be able to tell you what that prescription is for." Len pushed the boy forward.

JB handed over the piece of paper from Matty's wallet to him. The boy looked at it for a moment. "Well, it's no surprise you couldn't make this out. I can barely read it myself. I can see that this is one of two prescriptions and it's for Romazeapam."

"That much we got on our own. What the medication is for is what we need to know."

"Just a second. I'm looking it up." He flipped through the pages of his book. "Oh, okay, Romazeapam..." He fell silent as he read the entry, then said, "...it's a very very strong sedative. Of the opioid family. A narcotic. This prescription is for twenty pills. That would be the normal amount for a month or more."

"Would it be enough to cause death if they were taken all at once?"

"Of course. But who would do that?"

"What are you getting at, JB?"

"Do you remember the dead man's nail pads. They were blue. I've been wondering about that." He turned back to the student. "Could that blue be a result of an overdose of these pills?"

"Cyanosis of the fingers? Yeah, I suppose so. It's a symptom of at least one of the ingredients in the pills. But it would have to be a large dose."

"Like twenty pills all at once?" The boy nodded. "Okay, that answers one of my questions. Thanks." JB turned back to the bar and started to fiddle with Matty's addendum, flipping the pages back and forth as he checked dates.

Len sat next to him. "Uh, JB, can I talk to you?"

JB put the date book down. "I guess. What's up?"

Len went on to explain what Henry had presented him with. About the musical immortalizing vaudeville female impersonator Julian Eltinge.

"Wait a second. You're thinking of doing a musical about a drag queen? Where'd that come from?"

Len explained. "Remember, JB, I'm going to be out of work soon. With no prospects of anything else. Can't you see what a great idea it is? I would star. In drag, true. It isn't as if I've never worn a dress"****

"I know you said you wanted to come out publicly but this is pushing it a bit don't you think? Is running in the streets scaring the horses such a great idea? Wouldn't a press interview do the same thing?"

"Let's see. Over the years the press has said I'm flamboyant, sensitive, colorful, outrageous, irrepressible, effete, campy, effervescent, elfin, boyish, nervous, fabulous...." He shrugged. "All the usual code words. I'm pretty sure the public already has a very good idea of what I am."

"As to this musical, Len. If I remember my gay history correctly you're talking about playing a drag queen that went to great lengths to constantly declare his manhood far and wide. The man was closeted behind steel doors, Len. Julian Eltinge wasn't

****This part of Len's past can be read about in the 1st Bent Mystery, *Secrets Don't Belong In Closets.*

a very enlightened female impersonator was he?"

"That had more to do with the times he lived in, JB. The nineteenth century was one of the more unenlightened ones. Look at poor Oscar Wilde."

"And Eltinge killed himself in the 1940's. Gay history again. This is supposed to be a musical comedy, right?"

"Well, Henry did say there were some problems with the book. Maybe..."

"And I'll add my own say to that." JB held up a hand. "Len, don't you even think about asking me to help you with this. I have more than enough projects on my plate already. Besides you can't afford me."

"Well, then maybe I could take a stab at it myself."

JB sat back and appraised Len. Was this a reaction to his being offered that book deal? Didn't he realize the publishers only wanted one of those featherweight, cocktail kinds of biographies? Funny and scandalous stories about the theater. But then everybody always thinks they have a book in them. They think it's all bestsellers and book launch parties. Far be it from JB to crush any want-a-be writer's aspirations.

"Why not, Len? You want to write. Have a go at it. Now, can I get back to Matty's date book." JB turned away from Len and muttered to himself. "There's something in this thing I'm missing."

"Okay, then, JB, I will."

He stood to walk away, to leave JB to his own devices, when he ran right into Liam.

Len stopped him. "Sorry, Detective. It won't do any good to talk to JB right now. He's gone into one of his automaton modes. He gets like this every once in a while on every case. He'll sit there like a clockwork mouse running a maze while he puts all that he knows together in nice orderly rows. It's a part of his process. Very computer like. He makes CP3O look like Shecky Greene. You learn to live with it" He placed an arm on Liam's shoulder as he guided him away. "Let's leave him to his thinking, okay? But, Detective, let's you and me get to know each other a little bit better..."

If this man is going to become a fixture in JB's

orbit then Len—as JB's best friend—wanted to know something about him. Would the cop be all right for JB to hang around with? Is he a secret sociopath with social anxieties? A closet serial predator? Which didn't necessarily make him a bad person in Len's eyes, but Len wondered if he would even like this man? Would he fit in with the dynamic of their little group? Could he keep up with them? When JB and Len got going it could be hard to take in all at once,

These things were important to know since Len had observed so obvious a connection beginning between the two men.

# XXI

iam and Len sat together on one of the steps in the pit. Len grabbed a pillow and stuffed it behind his back, then wiggled a bit to get comfortable. He turned and faced the officer with one of his more serious expressions. "Now, do you want to explain what's going on here?"

"Sure. I'm trying to solve a murder."

"That's not what I meant and you know it. I mean what's up between you and JB. Fess up, Tiger Lily?"

Liam shrugged. He still wasn't getting what Len was aiming at. "He's been a big help so far." And a light finally went on. "But I take it that isn't what you mean. You're asking if we've become more than...well, I'll say colleagues, okay? It's only been a few hours you know?"

At least the detective doesn't have an IQ on the wrong side of a hundred, Len decided. He said to the cop, "Exactly. You see JB is my friend. And I'm quite aware of what's been going on here tonight. We've all heard of instant karma. John Lennon wasn't so off the mark was he? It really doesn't take all that long for two people to click."

"So it's your job to protect him is it?"

"Actually it is. Kinda. Without him knowing it, of course. I just know that JB has been known to be a bit foolish when he's enthralled with someone."

"And you think he's enthralled with me?"

"And you with him from all indications."

Liam shook his head. "No, that's not possible. Not yet. I just left another thing behind, and there is no way I'm ready to jump into anything else. I will admit to finding him...uh...interesting."

Len nodded agreement with Liam.

Liam held up his hand. "As a detective, I mean. He seems to take in all the little details. And he's very deductive in his way of thinking things through. You know the whole friggin' world has become so damned distracted of late. But that doesn't seem so true of JB. I watched him peel the skin off this case tonight, and it wasn't done in any conventional way. I find that... intriguing."

Len agreed with the detective. "I do know what you mean. You see JB tends to be somewhat isolated and shut down a lot of the time. He spends a whole lot of time inside his own head. Maybe its because he's alone in that apartment of his every day. It's just him and his little dog most of the time. It's these crimes and cases that pull him away from his solitary existence. They give him focus."

"Then I'm providing him a service by asking for his help."

I'm sure you can provide several services to our JB, Len was thinking. But there were still a couple of things he wanted to make clear to this very handsome policeman. "Detective, you need to know that JB is capable of a great deal of strength. I've seen it. There can even be a sort of gentle violence at moments When it's called for. But there is also a profound sense of humanity about him. He believes completely in fair play and honesty."

Liam mused, "I get that. I see a sensitivity in him. And a real cultured approach. But there are also a couple of small cracks in his facade. Those make it clear that there's real poetry in him. I suppose that's why he writes..." Liam stopped talking, realizing, perhaps, he'd given away feelings he wasn't quite ready to admit to.

Len smiled. "So you are attracted to him, aren't you? Well, trust me, he'll give your penis a nice cozy home."

Liam blushed a little at Len's remark. The freckles on his cheeks turned a soft pink. Well, well, Len was thinking, isn't that sweet? A person who can still blush. After living in New York as long as he had a rush of blood to his cheeks was only a sign of an oncoming hot flash.

Liam held up his hand. "Hold it there, Len. I have no idea if that's even where any of this might be headed. I guess we'll have to wait and see, won't we?"

"But you wouldn't be disappointed if something did come of it?"

"It's way to early to tell. I'll need to find out much more about him."

"Well, that might just work in your favor, because JB has always been far more questions than answers."

# XXII

rik could feel his skin crawling already. He was on his way down to the hot tub room to meet up with that Benny character. That grotesque little man who had the nerve to be trying to blackmail him over what he'd thought was a completely buried indiscretion in his past

Benny had shoved a note under the door of Erik's room saying he had pictures of Erik that he knew he would find "interesting" if not incriminating. Then the toad made mention of a time in Erik's past that he would have much rather have forgotten.

Erik had grown up in a medium sized town in California's San Fernando Valley. His father—that would be Gunnar's brother—had settled in the West when he'd immigrated to the USA in the 1960s. His son, Erik, had been born after his arrival and grew up a West Coast kid with a sense of adventure and a bit of the old wanderlust. That was how he'd followed his inclinations and ended up in New York to be a model. It could just as easily have been Los Angeles or London or Paris. Or Oshkosh. Anywhere there was money to be made from his looks and an opportunity for Erik to get his share of it.

Back at the beginning of his journey, in that medium-sized town, there hadn't been all that much for a kid to do. That is until Erik had discovered there existed in his burg an underground gay scene that he'd found youthfully fascinating. Eventually he would go so far as to join a local bar drag show and lip-sync to records as Helen Heels.

Now here was this Benny troll saying he had pictures from back then, and that he wasn't averse to making them available to the tabloid rags he worked for. Erik needed to get those pictures back. He was prepared to do whatever was called for to accomplish that.

Benny had arrived early to the Jacuzzi room because he had a little prep work to do before his target of the evening arrived for their assignation. He hadn't planned on doing this tonight, but seeing Erik sitting in the bar when he'd first arrived made him whip up a new plan for his evening at the tubs.

It wouldn't be the first time Benny had been down this particular road. He lived by a credo that he should get his rocks off anywhere or anytime an opportunity presented itself. And he wasn't the least bit choosy about who he got it off with. Fatties. Oldies. Gimps. Geeks. He just seldom got a chance at the pretty ones. For Benny all were welcome. He couldn't afford to reject anyone. He had to be a sexual carnivore. He knew he wasn't an attractive man. He'd heard the terrible thing's men said behind his back. But he wasn't going to let that keep him from engaging in all the sex he could find. If for no other reason, as revenge for the pain inflicted. And living in New York it had turned out that his opportunities were substantial.

He'd found that with a black hood over his face and a hard won gym body in tight leather pants with a bulging crotch he could attract any number of men on a Saturday night at *The Anvil* or *The Spike*, two of the more popular S&M bars down in the Village. For Benny sex was a weapon wielded indiscriminately. But those real beauties—the one's like Erik—they tended to elude his wide spread nets. He'd cure that oversight tonight.

"Okay, where are the pictures?" Erik wasn't in any mood for fun and games, he only wanted to get this whole distasteful thing over with.

Benny huffed, "I don't have them with me, ya bloody sod. I think we needs to talk first."

"This isn't a social call, Benny. What the hell do you want?"

Benny wrung his hands together as if he were some old time melodrama villain. "What I had in mind is way more social than that, beautiful man."

Erik sighed. This wasn't the first time a man had come on to him, but he had to admit it had never happened with this particular set of circumstances in play. Nor from anyone quite so disgusting as Benny. Or from someone who held such a strong hand over his head. Erik resigned himself to paying Benny's tariff, whatever it might cost him. "So, you'll give me the pictures if we get...what did you call it...*social* right here and now?"

Benny felt his cock filling with blood, getting him semi-hard, which the towel he had wrapped around him did little to hide. He looked Erik up and down and felt the blood also rush to that other sex organ—his brain. Quarts of endorphins and testosterone became a potent mix of sexual desire and lust rushing from his head. He didn't say a word. He knew he didn't have to. He had his own ace-for-the-hole—you should pardon the expression.

He removed the towel and that covered him and posed. Showing off his rock hard abs, his chiseled chest, his hard flexing arm's, and his twelve and one-half inch cock, waving in the air like a 4th of July flag. The one all the gay size queens practically came just from looking.

Erik's eyes grew wide as he went to his knees in front of the little man. "My God, that thing is huge.

That's way out of proportion to your size, man."

Benny chucked. "They don't call me Beercan Benny for no reason, mate."

Before long Erik's jaw was aching from the stretching it had been subjected to while sucking Benny's gigantic cock. The back of his throat was raw from the head of Benny's dick pounding on the tender flesh there.

Then Benny—who was seeing this as an encounter rather than the rape that Erik was thinking it was—took hold of Erik's shoulders and stood him up, he removed his towel and stepped in close to him. He rose on his toes and began to kiss and suck and tongue the beautiful man's chest and nibs, trailing through the line of hair that led to his groin. Giving him slippery but sensual pleasure, causing Erik to moan with the sensation. Then Benny bent only slightly and began reciprocating on Erik for his hard work before. As practiced as he was in the art of sex, he knew how to turn men on. In fact, much of his own pleasure came from the giving as from the getting. He went on to give Erik a prolonged sucking with some light ball play to add an element of sweet pain. When that had Erik squirming and moaning under his saliva filled mouth Benny gently led Erik to lie down on a close by bench. He moved between Erik's thighs to nuzzle in close against his backside. Then he bent to suckle at Erik's butt cheeks, moving side to side. He lightly slapped at them until they turned a sweet warm pink. At that his head finally went to Erik's darkest spot. He spent a long time tonguing and fingering his sphincter, rimming there until taut muscles relaxed and Erik begged Benny to fuck him. Benny always insisted on that. His partners had to ask him to penetrate them.

It was when Erik was lying on the bench with his legs held high in the air, Benny deep inside him, that it happened.

Benny was in tight to his ass, his engorged

cock filling him, touching him in places that had never been touched before, ramming Erik hard...that was when he heard the pop and saw the flash.

He was looking through half-closed eyes, awash with the feelings Benny's pounding was bringing up in him, when he registered the exploding light as a kind of fireworks going off in his fogged out head. Weren't the chrysanthemum puffs great!? Then his real brain took over and asked, "What the hell?"

He lifted his head and looked around, then looked at Benny. "What the hell have you done?" He scrambled to pull away and get to his feet, leaving Benny's hard dick to again wave in the air.

Erik spun around to look for himself where the flash he'd seen had come from. It was there. From the rack of towels beside the door to the steam room.

Erik went to the rack and lifted the towels until he found Benny's camera hidden behind them. The camera with the professional flash. The one that obviously had a remote switch that Benny was holding in his hand to operate.

Erik took the few steps needed to hover menacingly over the little son of a bitch.

Benny was still on his knees with his half-hard dick in his hand thinking maybe Erik was planning to put his Johnson up his Jacksie. But the look on Erik's face was telling him something different. He stammered, "Hey, come on, mate, it weren't nothing. For me own personal use." He reached out to run a hand over Erik's chest. "I want to remember this, luv. You are so foikin' gorgeous."

But Erik wasn't having it.

It was at that moment that Benny finally saw the menacing and very ugly impulse Erik was barely holding inside himself. Erik's voice was as cold as a winter bear's growl as he said "You were going to use this against me, weren't you?" He shook the camera he'd grabbed over Benny's head. "Sure. You make your sleazeball living being a dirty blackmailer. It's what you do. You don't know any better. But you know what? I don't think you should get away with it anymore."

Benny scuttled backward, moving back and away from Erik. There was real fear in his eyes. By now Benny had seen something even more venomous and evil in Erik's face. A threat that Benny didn't think he could talk his way out of. Erik was foikin' mad. Erik was lookin' foikin' crazy. Bloody foikin' bollocks, Erik was coming toward him.

# XXIII

he scream reverberated through the Atrium as if Irish banshee were working overtime. Standing from their seats in the pit both Len and Liam shouted, "What the hell was that!" JB rushed to the bar entrance from inside and asked, "Who screamed?" The two men shrugged at him.

A staff member came out of the office to rush by.

"What was that?" Liam yelled to the boy's rapidly retreating figure.

He turned and kept running, only backward. "It came from the Jacuzzi area. Over there." He pointed to the other side of the pit. Then he turned around to keep going toward the sound.

JB and Dimity left the bar together, with Liam and Len both joining them. In a tuna like group they started toward the area the staff guy had indicated was the direction of the scream.

As they passed by the showers a naked and dripping Erik came to the entrance. The man really was a blatant exhibitionist. It wasn't as if he didn't have anything to show off. He did. A perfect swimmer toned body and an appreciable member between his legs. It's just that there is a time and place, for God's sake.

Dimity said, "Cover yourself, you idiot. This ain't the Pussycat Theater, fer crips sake. You ain't no go-go boy." She moved on.

Erik put his hands over his crotch to cover up. The man was pretty and able to follow orders—that could make him very popular with a certain segment of the gay population, Len speculated.

Erik shouted to the group as it passed by, "What's going on? Where's everybody going?"

Len answered him as he went by. "There was a noise from the hot tub area. We're going to find out what it was."

Erik reached behind him to grab a towel from the rack there. Wrapping it at his waist he took off after the rest of the crowd. Following closely on his heels was Henry, who had come down from upstairs to join in the exodus.

They all crowded into the doorway of the hot tub room but went no farther. They were stopped cold by what they saw in that room. Shocked expressions quickly replaced the questioning ones that had been there moments before. Dimity, going all girly again, turned away and covered her mouth—mainly to  curb her reaction to the scene laid out before them. Not such a tough guy after all she struggled to stifle herself. What wasn't completely clear was what her reaction would be. Was she going to gag or scream?

JB and Liam were the first of the group to recover themselves. They both stepped into the room to join the staff guy kneeling at edge of the pool.

The tub's jets were on full, roiling the water into soft waves lapping against the rim of the concrete pit. A thin bubbling foam had formed on the surface of the water, which was tinted a soft pink from the blood flowing from the body spread eagled face down in the water.

Erik, from the doorway, asked in a shaken voice, "Is he dead?"

Dimity swung on him. Her questioned reaction to the body turned out to be anger instead of fear. "Of course he's dead, you ignoramus," she snapped. "How could he not be with all that blood? Just keep quiet won't you?" She turned back to ask. "Who is it, JB?"

Seeing no other way to find out, JB slipped into the water and swam over to the body. Taking hold of the arm he lifted, which served to turn the dead man over to bobble face up. JB shouted to the group. "It's Benny. That photographer guy. And he is dead."

JB again took hold of the little man's arm so he could pull him to the outer edge of the pool where Liam and the staff guy, both still kneeling there, grabbed at his body. With some effort they pulled Benny out to lie like a hooked carp on the wet concrete surround.

Liam quickly examined the body. "He was hit with something. There's a large gash on his forehead."

Len, now standing over the two men, added his own observation. "Along with a huge dick. I mean will you look at that thing. No wonder Benny was always slouched over." He looked around the small room. "I'll bet you my Aunt Tillie's recipe for elderberry wine that Benny was hit with that." He pointed to a damaged camera thrown under a slatted bench over by the wall. It was the same camera that Benny had been using when Len had confronted him in his room. Now, however, the flash attachment was bent in half. There were also traces of blood on the metal surface.

"Whoever did this used Benny's own camera to kill him. They must have grabbed it away from him and then smashed it on his head. At least a couple of times it looks like. That's cold, man."

Liam stood and said to the staff guy. "Can we get a sheet to cover the body?" He went off to get one. Liam then turned to the group of people still standing in the doorway. "I would like all of you to move back out to the lobby," he directed. "Actually, if you would all go down into the pit it would be better. Now please." He ended his order with a clenched smile, "And if any one of you move from there I swear I'll have you charged and arrested. So move it. Go on."

They moved.

He turned back to JB, who was now out of the water and bending over Benny's body. "This is so strange, Detective. What possible connection could Benny have with Matty Silverman?"

"You think the two killings are connected? This isn't two separate crimes then?"

"Well, that would mean that we have two killers among us. Isn't that a comforting thought?"

"I see what you mean. Well, maybe we should go talk to our little group and get this straightened out."

They left Benny to make his dark journey to whatever fate awaited him.

Despite the ongoing problem that his voice garnered little respect at the best of times Liam was more than capable of taking charge when called upon. And it was certainly called for in this instance. Pitching his voice to a lower register and using his sternest tone he first spoke with the three Atrium staff people.

"I want you guys to do a complete search of the building. Take a peek into every kink room, every glory hole, and every dark corner this place has. Anybody you find you bring them out here to the pit right away. I want every breathing body in this place sitting in this hole. Pronto. Capiche?" They nodded. "Also, I need you to use your master keys and open up every door and every locker in the entire place. Even the storage room doors. And leave them open. I'm going to call my precinct and get me some backup. They'll be put to work thoroughly searching this place. Now go."

He turned back to the small group sitting on the steps of the pit.

JB asked, "Getting backup, huh? Won't that just confuse things?"

"Besides," Len sniggered. "That's sounds distinctly like some kind of gay slur, doesn't it, JB? You want *backup* do you? Here? In a gay baths? Really?" He grinned at his witticism.

Liam snorted derisively. "Not at all. But you're going to get my back up if you don't sit down and shut the hell up."

Len did as he was told.

# XXIV

rik and Henry were the only ones in the group that Liam didn't know of their whereabouts when Benny screamed his last. The rest of them—JB, Len, Dimity, and himself—were all in or around the bar area when they'd heard it. So, for his first move, Liam decided to get those two missing people placed. He stepped down into the pit so he was closer and wouldn't have to shout. The lower register he was using to issue orders was rough on his throat.

Erik said he was taking a shower. Len collaborated his story, having passed him on the way to the hot tub. Henry said he had been in his room. He'd heard Benny's howl echo from there.

"Which room is yours," Liam asked.

"Number one-oh-two. At the top of the balcony."

"Okay, you come with me then. I want to search your room." Henry stood. "The rest of you yahoos stay here." Liam started to climb the steps then turned back, "JB, keep an eye on them."

Liam and Henry went off together toward the

upstairs area.

Henry opened the door to his room and stood aside so the Detective could go in on his own. He stood in the doorway to watch.

"What is it you're looking for, Officer?"

Liam shrugged. "I'll know it when I see it."

Really, he didn't have a clue what he was looking for. Anything that might incriminate Henry in the crime was the general idea. But he had no idea what that might be. Plus, he was pretty sure most anything he did find wouldn't hold up in court since there wasn't a warrant anywhere near his looking around. But Henry was being so cooperative it only made sense to take advantage of it.

Liam checked out the cubical. Henry was one of those neat and tidy types. His gold lamé jacket from the show was hung carefully on a hanger along with the rest of his costume. His shoes were neatly placed under the shelf by the cot. On the shelf was a file folder. Liam sat on the cot and opened it. It held the sheet music used in Dimity's act. He turned to face the door prepared to ask Henry a question. It died when he heard the crinkle of paper coming from somewhere under him. He wondered, what the hell that was?

He stood and picked up a corner of the mattress. What he found was a piece of paper. Folded and creased into a square about three inches on each side.

"What's this?" Liam picked up the note and held it up so that Henry could see it.

Henry shook his head. "I couldn't guess, Detective. I've never seen that before."

Liam opened it and scanned the contents. Then slowly read the typed letter to himself. It read:
Gunnar:

I found out I'll need to go before you. I will not linger here. I'll wait for you wherever I end up.
Jag, lskar dig, min alska, min kinderstrudle.
It was hand signed: *Matty Silverman.*

Well, Liam realized, this reads suspiciously like a

suicide note. But if Silverman killed himself then why did he suffer that gunshot wound to his head? This case was having way to many twists for his comfort.

"What does it say, Detective?" Henry was still standing in the doorway watching the officer.

"Huh? Oh, I don't think it's anything that concerns you, Henry. You're okay for the moment, but there's something I have to do downstairs." He took a step toward the doorway. "You should follow me down."

Once on the lobby floor Liam went directly to the bar, leaving Henry to return to the pit to sit with the others. Once there Liam took his own look at Matty Silverman's agenda. He flipped the pages as he looked for someplace that Matty had signed his name. He finally found it on an old receipt tucked in the pocket at the back. It matched the signature on the note. That settled it. Matty Silverman wasn't murdered after all. He'd killed himself. But that raised the question of who had then gone into his cubical and mutilated his dead body? Who had tried to make his suicide look like a murder? And why? The case had taken another turn.

"So it was a B-F-T that killed Benny, right?"

"A what?"

"A B-F-T. Blunt Force Trauma."

"Len, the police call a blunt force trauma a blunt force trauma. You've been watching too many episodes of *Murder She Wrote* on TV. Why don't we let the coroner do his job this time around. He'll decide what killed Benny. After he does his autopsy."

"Come on, JB. We both know his head was caved in with that camera we found. What I'm wondering is why? Benny was a P-I-T-A, but he didn't deserve that."

"He was a what?"

"A P-I-T-A. A Pain In The Ass."

JB smiled. "O...kay. I'll give you that this time. Although this whole acronym thing you've got going can get O-R-S."

"O-R-S?"

"Old Real Soon. So, what were you and the detective talking about?"

"Oh, you saw that did you?"

"I don't miss much, Len. It's an ability that comes in handy when you're trying to solve crimes."

"We were just talking..."

"About what, pray tell?" JB's question was sharp—opening envelope's sharp.

Len effected a light tone. "Oh, we were talking about moons and Junes and Ferris wheels..."

"You were playing mother hen again weren't you? Over me seeing Liam?" JB crossed his arms over his chest. "Since when do I need your approval of who I choose to be with?"

"You don't. But I wanted to get to know him a little if he's going to be around. He is isn't he?"

"There is a possibility. And what is your decision about him?"

"Well, he's way better than that Toby was.**** At least this guy is old enough to get into an R-rated movie without having to show his ID."

"So you approve of him? Great. I'm so relieved to have your approval, especially when you consider the most excitement in my life lately is no heartburn after dinner. Len, I'm only looking to add some zippity to my doo-da, as you quaint Southerner's are apt to say."

"Hey, I get it, your lonely, but watch it when you start bashing on the South, fella." He raised a single finger. "We will rise again. All over you if needs be." Len smiled. "So go ahead, see the guy, JB. Go crazy. I've always been of the opinion that if anyone manages to find someone to love they should be happy...and in your case, extremely grateful."

JB made a swacking sound to mimic getting hit in the chest with an arrow. Len snickered under his breath. That zinger would serve to get JB back for that tacky remark earlier. Now, they were even again. "And, by

****JB's affair with Toby is chronicled in the 2nd Bent Mystery, *A Murderous Ball Of Fluff.*

the way, you missed my Joni Mitchell reference there. I thought it was pretty fey if I don't say so myself."

"What? You mean I missed a song clue? You should take away my gay card."

"Hey." Len swung his hand back and forth pendulum style. "What's with the rotten mood and lousy tude, chum?"

"Um, sorry. It's just there's something about this case that I'm not getting. I'm not seeing it. And it's making me nuts. I swear I'm at the point where I don't know whether to check my ass or scratch my watch. Or is that more Southern bashing?"

Len broke up—which was the point of the bickering between the two to begin with. Whichever of them got the most laughs won. He decided to give up on this session of sniping between them and offered his version of an olive branch. "JB, I swear you are just the height of too-muchery. I think I'd miss you even if we'd never met." He paused a moment. "Uh, can I bother you about something?"

"Considering our history I'm sure you will," JB answered, getting in one last barb. "What is it?"

"It's about Benny. I know the little hobbit was a leach and a parasite. Or are they the same thing?" He thought about that for a second. "Oh, well, it doesn't matter, does it? What I'm getting at here is there have to be a multitude of reasons to not care about Benny dying the way he did. But that scene in the hot tub was way out of line with his irritant factor. It was downright brutal. I'm thinking whoever did it was way out of control to kill him like that."

"You may be right, Len. It did look like a crime of the moment to me too. It was probably not premeditated. It was done in a sort of frenzy."

"And I want to know who it was that did it. Because that kind of behavior truly scares the crap out of me."

"Len, I don't know if I can help you tonight. I'm still on this thing with Matty Silverman."

"What if I do it, JB. How about I go after the one that killed Benny. Okay? I think I can do it, JB."

"Well, I guess you don't need my permission, Len.

Go ahead, knock yourself out."

"But I could possibly maybe need some help. I don't have a lot of experience with this sort of thing. Like you do."

"Don't be silly, Len. You've helped me on every one of the cases I've managed to solve. Come on, you know as much about this detecting game as I do. You've been terrific as someone to bounce ideas off of."

"Then that's what I'll need, is it? A listener."

"Sure. A Mr. Laurel to your Mr. Hardy."

"But who?"

"How about her?" JB pointed at Dimity.

"Don't you mean Hardy to my Laurel?"

"Why not use Dimity? You could be a like a comedy duo . Abbott and Costello. Martin and Lewis

"The plague and Europe?"

"Well, you two seem to get along pretty well, although it does remind me of something out of a George Baxt mystery novel. Pharoah Love meets Mrs. Plotkin"

"Ha. I know what you mean. He can write em', can't he? See, JB, I know who you're talking about. I read books too. I know what it takes to write one."

JB looked at Len closely. So he wants to talk about this book deal of his right now does he? Well, all right then.

"And you think that's all it takes to make you a writer, do you? Len, there's way more to it than knowing basic story structure. Trust me, I know from where I speak."

"Well, you had to start somewhere, JB. You must have sat down one day and wrote out your first page. I think I deserve a chance to do the same thing."

"And I wouldn't think of stopping you. But listen here. I categorically refuse to teach you how to write. I won't play Dashiell Hammett to your Lillian Hellman. So don't even ask. Go to the New School and take a course if you want lessons."

"Right. I will then." Len was agreeing but the look on his face showed he was hurt by JB's bluntness.

JB saw the look and took a little pity on him. He said,

"But here's an idea for right now. A test of sorts. You were telling me about this musical that Henry's writing. The problem, as I see it, is you have a main character that kills himself in the end. Which isn't exactly an uplifting climax for a musical comedy. Why don't you write a better ending for your libretto. I'll even read the first draft of it, if you want me to. So there you go, Len. I've done my bit. Now, what were you planning to do about Dimity?"

"Well, I think you've had a good idea. I'll think on it." Len smiled.

JB stood and wiped at the seat of his towel. Len remained seated. JB looked down at him. "So, when?" He jerked his head in Dimity's direction.

"Oh, you meant now?" He paused a second. "Well, okay. I guess I'll ask her right now."

# XXV

Dimity balked at first. She couldn't see any valid reason for looking into Benny's messy demise. "He was an intrusive little worm. Every time I got around him I felt like I needed a shower. Frankly, I don't really care who did him in." Poor Benny. He turned out to be a perfect example of reaping what you've sown.

"But Dimity," Len cajoled. "You have to understand. Benny's death means there's someone on these premises right now that has murdered another person. Who do you think he'll go after next? Could it be me? Could it be you?"

She stood. "All right. You win. You have a valid point. I really don't want to get killed here tonight. Can you see the headlines that would make?" She held up her hand and swept it across the air. "DIVA DROWNED IN TUBS. Too tacky. So whatta you want we should do?"

"Why don't we check out the murder scene first."

"But that cop said we're supposed to stay here."

"Hey, do you see him here? He didn't even follow his

own orders did he? If that's the case why should we?"

Dimity tilted her head, thinking a moment, then gave in. "Fine." She waved her hands. "Onward, fearless leader."

The two climbed the steps out of the pit and headed back to the hot tub room.

Once they were next to the Jacuzzi Len pulled the sheet half away from Benny's corpse. When Len had seen his body before there was a certain degree of repugnance at seeing the man dead, but now, after some time had passed, his body had become merely a carcass, a shell. It was only the vessel that had held Benny's spirit, and that spirit had long since departed. Benny's container no longer held for Len any emotion except absence.

It wasn't the same for Dimity. The girl really was turning out to be a total wimpette, all mushy and soft on the inside. And quite often on the outside too. When Len pulled back the sheet from Benny's body Dimity gulped and turned away from the sight of him. "Oh, crap," she cried. She threw an arm over her eyes to block the sight of him from her view.

Meaning to quickly back out of the small room, and away from Benny, she blindly stumbled backward to end up groping at the door she found stopping her retreat.

"It isn't a good idea to go in there, Dimity. That's the door to the steam room. It could be a total shock for one or two of your sensitivities, it'll fizzle your hair, and there's all that wayward conduct you might see."

"Damn…" She backed away again, this time to get away from the door. She was stopped when she ran up against Benny's rigor stiffened and unmoving legs. She peeked through opened fingers and exclaimed, "Oh, shit!" She spun around and tiptoed backward now with her hands held to her mouth to keep herself from squealing. There was actually a pretty good reason for her reaction.

In death all of Benny's muscles had relaxed to hang like sets of old drapes off the sides of his tiny frame. The skin of his face especially had sunk away from the bones of his skull. The cheeks had sunk inward, making bony caves under his eyes. His eyelids were two slits, half open, so Benny's eyeballs stared out from the recessed sockets. His lips had pulled away from his teeth so he seemed to grin maniacally in the rigor of his death. His hands were two claws crossed like a pirate's symbol across his chest. Len was reminded of the pictures *National Geographic* always show of two hundred year old mummified Tibetan monks found in remote caves in the Himalayas. Benny looked like an escapee from Shangri-La.

"My God." Dimity gulped, "He's the only dead person I've ever seen outside of a funeral home. I didn't know death could be so cruel." She wiped at her eyes.

"Yep. It is, hon. But why the tears? You certainly didn't like Benny when he was alive. And death doesn't change what he was, sister. Benny wasn't a very nice man."

"It isn't that. It's that smell. What is that? It's so strong. Like cat piss."

Dimity was right. But what she was smelling wasn't from any feline. It was the odor of human urine. It filled the muggy air of the hot tub room with its rank odor. Len guessed that Benny must have had a full bladder when he went into the pool. In death his body had let go and expelled the water he'd been holding. The hot tub filter hadn't been able to clear it completely yet.

"Just another of death's happy effects, Dimity. That's the reason morticians make such a good living. They make their customers all pretty for the grieving mourners. Although, I don't think Benny will have many of those."

Len bent to examine Benny's head. Out of the water the wound that marred his forehead had begun to coagulate. Its edges looked raw and red, reminding Len of a butcher's sirloin. It was a deep cut that had caved in the right side of Benny's skull.

"I was right, the wounds he suffered were really violent. Whoever did this used a huge amount of force. I'd say the attacker was, at the least, royally pissed off at our Benny, if he wasn't bordering on outright crazy. I wonder what Benny did to deserve this kind of violence?"

"What's that?" Dimity was pointing into the pool.

"Where?" Len stood. "What do you see?"

"Down there, at the bottom. Something shiny."

Len moved to the edge of the pool. "You're right. What is that?"

Dimity stood beside Len. "I'll bet its jewelry of some kind. I have a built in radar for that kind of thing. Shiny objects will always get my attention."

"I've heard that sharks have that same ability."

"And exactly what are you implying, bub?"

"Absolutely nothing. It's just a piece of completely superfluous information." He wisely held back on his opinion that silvery gray was a color best banned from her wardrobe. "Totally unrelated to anything to do with you."

"In that case, go get it."

"If I must..."

"Of course you must. It might be something important. A real clue."

Len sat on the edge of the hot tub and slipped into the water. As he moved against the current the towel wrapped at his waist loosened and floated away. He got to the center, bent under, and came up with the object in his hand.

It was a watch. An expensive watch from the looks of it. All heavy and chrome with a link bracelet for a band.

Len made his way back over to the side and handed it up to Dimity. She took it from him and examined it like a jeweler making an appraisal. She held it to her nose and squinted at it through slanted eyes.

Len, still bobbing in the hot tub water, asked her, "Uh, sweetie, could you get me a towel? From the wall over there. Please? Otherwise I will have to flash my private's at you."

Dimity smiled. "Not such an unpleasant prospect. I bet Benny would have loved it. It would be a bare-assed picture made for the tabloids." She went to the shelf over at the side to grab him a towel. "And its not like I haven't seen naked men before. Look at where I'm work. I see more men's dicks than a peeper in a monastery from the stage every night. Twice on Thursdays and Sundays."

"Well, you haven't seen *my* penis, and I'd like to keep it that way, thank you."

She laughed and handed Len the towel, then bent again to the watch she was still holding. "Len, this wrist watch. It's Matty's. I'd know it anywhere. He wore it all the time. His lover gave it to him."

"Are you sure?" She nodded. "Then that means Benny's death and Matty's are connected somehow. But how is that possible?"

Len noticed that still wrapped around Benny's wrist was his room key. He climbed from the water, quickly draped the towel Dimity had given him at his waist, and bent at Benny's side. Using a finger on each side of the corpses' wrist he stretched the elastic cord as gingerly as he could to slide the key up and over Benny's bony fingers. Len stood. "We need to go to Benny's room, Dimity. Maybe we'll find our answer there."

Len covered Benny's body with the sheet again.

Dimity asked, "How are we going to get upstairs, Len? That cop wanted us to stay in the pit. We're not supposed to be wandering all over the building."

"If we take the stairs at this end of the lobby we should be safe. Sneaking up those we won't have to pass by the pit and risk being caught."

The two went out of the hot tub room and slunk to the rear stairs. Both of them bent low to make themselves as small a target as possible, then quickly went up. They must have had luck on their side because no one yelled at them to return to the pit.

They arrived on the second floor in only a minute.

# XXVI

heir assent actually didn't go unnoticed. JB saw them going up the stairs but really didn't care all that much what it was they were up to. He didn't care even if they wanted to do laps around the balcony with sparklers alight. His head was to busy pondering over what he knew so far about Matty's Silverman's death. He knew there was something about it he wasn't seeing. But he just couldn't get a grip on what it might be.

A lot of what was bothering him was that gunshot to Matty's face. It was total overkill. If Matty had taken sleeping pills previously how could the man with a gun not have seen that Matty was at the least groggy? He would have been that if he hadn't been already dead when his killer arrived. So, why shoot him? Overkill.

What JB was really questioning was why Matty would want to kill himself to begin with? What unbearable thing had caused him to want to give up on his life? From all indications he appeared to have a successful career. His relationship was stable, although in some distress at the moment. Or was that it? Was that the catalyst? The trigger that tipped the scales?

Did Matty's wish to die have something to do with Gunnar, his lover, being ill? Maybe Matty had received news that his lover was going to die soon? Gunnar was currently in a hospital with something considered incurable. If that dire prognosis was the case then Matty taking his own life would begin to make some sense. That is if you looked at the situation with a romantic predilection

JB was well aware that there are no worse romantics than gay men. Many of us feel a real need for all that operatic drama in our lives. What if Matty didn't want to continue his own life without his lover by his side? Melodramatic as it may sound there were several cases the last few years where two gay lovers had made suicide pacts between them. The NY Times had reported on a gay couple only the week before. They had gone over their balcony overlooking Park Avenue to fall seventeen floors together. This was because both of them had received an AIDS diagnoses from their doctors. Without a cure for the disease anywhere on the horizon people deciding to die before it had completely debilitated them wasn't such a crazy idea at that. At least you would make a pretty corpse. You could die with a smile on your face. Although there could be a little drool on your chin depending on what pills you might have used to off yourself.

JB realized he needed to fill in a bunch more information about Matty before any of this began to make any sense to him.

That was why he stood from where he was sitting in the pit, and like the others not following the detective's edict, left the pit to pursue his own errand. He went to the office window to check the clock there for the time. It was after 7AM.

He asked the clerk inside if he could use his phone to call that doctor Matty had listed in his agenda. The one who was his lover's physician. The same one Matty visited the day before he died. He needed to know if that visit was for the lover or for Matty himself?

XXVII

Dimity and Len found that Benny's room was a reflection of his life—messy and unkempt. Even in the tiny area provided Benny had managed to stuff it with crap that only Benny would have found valuable or needed.

"Jesus H. Christ. What a dump," Dimity said. She put her hands on her hips and made tsking noises as she scrutinized the cot. It was piled high with crumpled food and candy wrappers. Also there were a few wadded tissues that there was no way Dimity was touching, along with a couple of shoeboxes stuffed with papers. All of it was mixed together with a twisted cotton sheet and the suitcase that held all of Benny's photography equipment.

Len—who had been the first one in the room— knelt to rummage the little table by the side of the bed. He found a partly filled cold cup of coffee with two cigarette butts floating in it, a bottle of poppers, a tube of lube, a couple of condom packages, and a box of tissues. The man was prepared to mix work and pleasure evidently.

Len said to Dimity. "One of the first things JB taught me about this detecting gig was that you should always respect the dead person's spirit. He told me that keeping the noise level down would do that. Of course, I suspect he said it as a way to keep me quiet while he was thinking. I have to admit it isn't such a bad idea at that."

Dimity flipped him a dainty one fingered bird then gingerly made a space for herself on the cot to sit. She pulled one of the shoeboxes onto her lap. "What are we looking for here, anyway, Len? This is looking to be a needle and haystack situation."

Len, who was still considering if anything on the table could be the clue he was looking for, answered her. "The circumstances of Benny's death have got me wondering if he might have been killed by someone he was extorting for money. Money is always a convenient motive, right? Look at it this way. Someone in the baths tonight has to be the culprit. Now Benny's whole existence depended on the information he'd gathered, right? No matter how nefariously he may have gathered it. What if Benny had the goods on someone here tonight? Someone he was threatening to expose? What we might be looking for here would be any thing that might indicate who it was he was trying to blackmail."

"Again, its needles and straw, Len. It could be anything." She used two fingers to shift some of the papers in Benny's shoebox. "And remember Benny has his car on the parking lot downstairs. That's a bigger mess than this room."

Len spied Benny's overcoat hanging from the wall hook. It was cut from heavy black wool and had multiple pockets sewn into it. Len took it down from the wall. He sat beside Dimity and started to poke around in the inside breast pockets. "Benny was a lot of unpleasant things, but he was also methodical and a bit of a paranoid personality. I'm guessing he would have hidden any evidence he might have had on somebody. I learned this trick from JB a few months ago.****

Len spread the coat out over his knees and began

to run a hand over the inside. "Sometimes people hide their secrets in the linings of their coats." He ran a hand up inside the right sleeve. "I heard of one family that found a diamond necklace their deceased mother had hid in the lining of her winter coat." He shifted to the

****The trick can be found in *Secrets Don't Belong In Closets*, the 1st Bent Mystery

next sleeve. "Even JB and I found some film that helped solve a case we were working on once." He reached in to slide his hand around the collar. He smiled at Dimity. "Well, well. It looks as if Benny must have done something similar."

He asked Dimity if she had any scissors handy. She handed over a pair of the manicure type she kept in the fanny pac hanging at her waist. Another tacky accessory Len noted. He really needed to talk to her about her fashion choices.

Len took the little scissors and snipped at the stitches of the lining.

Soon enough he pulled out a small white envelope. It contained three pictures. Len looked at them closely and chuckled.

"Well, these have to be the holy grail of blackmailing material. Take a look." He handed the pictures to Dimity.

She looked at them, then let out a loud whoop. Hooting at what they showed. As she laughed she fell backward onto the mattress, chortling giddily, while kicking both feet in the air.

So much for respecting the dignity of Benny's death.

# XXVIII

 hey all heard the Atrium's speaker system snap on. Then came a tap, tap, tap from a finger, and then Liam's squeaky voice saying, "Is this on?...Yeah? Okay...Listen up people. I made it perfectly clear that I wanted all of you to keep your bony asses confined to the pit. You have two minutes to get back to this lobby and seated where I can see you. Or you'll be spending the rest of the morning at Rikers Island. Get back here...now!" As he said this his voice rose in timber until at the end his emphatic *now!* was so high only bats could have heard it.

Len stood. "I guess we'd better get back. Come on Dimity."

"I was putting my clothes on. Why is that such a big deal?" Erik huffed some, then went down the steps and sat next to Henry.

JB came from the direction of the office. "I was only making a phone call. But I'm going to need you to help me get what I need."

Liam didn't say anything but simply pointed downward. JB took a seat on one of the steps in the pit.

Len and Dimity arrived to slip by Liam guiltily. They sat with the rest, who now numbered about a dozen people.

The three staff guys had finished their search of the building and had ferreted out a pair of S&M types, both of them clad in black leather assless chaps with zippered hoods over their heads. Along with them was an older man they had found asleep in the baby room. He wore an adult diaper and a large plastic pacifier around his neck. Whatever butters your fly, right?

Liam motioned to the sergeant—the one who had originally been stationed at the front entrance. Liam's now ex-boyfriend—They spoke for a moment, both of them seeming agitated with the other. Then the uniformed cop turned and stomped off to return to his post out in the lobby. His departure whittled the group down to eleven.

Next Liam's discussion with the two leather men and the baby man had the three of them skittering up the stairs and checking out of the building within minutes. That reduced the group to nine.

The three staff guys, including Brian the bartender, were sent back to the office. Liam now had the group to a core of five.

JB, Len, Dimity, Henry, and Erik sat together as Liam looked them over. He knew that one or maybe two of them were his culprits. His killers. Either it was a single one of them who had murdered both Matty and Benny, or each of the dead men had a different killer. It was up to him—and any powers of detection he might have—to figure out which scenario was the one that had actually occurred.

At first Liam had thought that Benny was his man. He'd initially focused on him and went to some lengths to make him fit the circumstances of the crime. Liam felt that Benny had all the necessary requirements of a gunman for hire, which was his first idea about how the killing was accomplished. He was thinking Gunnar hired his own personal hitman from his hospital bed. Benny was obviously hungry for cash. His job clearly indicated that. Benny was also a loner, always keeping to himself. And the man did come off as a little weird. Was he ruthless enough to do the job? Liam still wanted the victim's lover hiring someone to kill Silverman for the insurance money, and Benny had fit the profile, damn it.

So it came as absolutely no help when JB pointed out that it was unlikely for Benny to have done the crime because he didn't look anything like his Uncle Waldo.

Liam was perplexed by this total nonsequitur. "Who?"

"My Uncle Waldo. Now he would make a perfect hitman. He looks like a cross between Elmer Fudd and Curly of The Three Stooges. And timid. You know the type. Hitmen always look like a piece of day old milquetoast. That way they can meld into crowds and stay inconspicuous. But Benny was just strange enough to stand out in any gathering. People backed away from him in abhorrence. He wasn't the hitman type."

Len said, "Then again, a killer for hire must have a layer of kink underneath it all. So they can do the deed. I always suspected The Three Stooges of a pronounced S&M inclination. All that eye gouging and forehead bashing. Very kinky that."

JB completely put an end to Liam's idea when he added, "Besides, Officer, Benny didn't arrive here at the Atrium until after Matty Silverman was already dead. So he couldn't possibly have done it."

That fact alone meant Liam had to search elsewhere for his killer. He wasn't thinking it was JB or Len, although he couldn't completely remove them from his suspect list. However, since neither of them had any reason to commit the crime he placed them at the bottom. They'd both made it clear that they didn't even know who Matty Silverman was until they'd met him that very night. And that went against rule number one in the murder book—the victim usually knows his killer.

Liam then was left with Henry, Erik and Dimity. He needed to break one of them.

With Benny now reluctantly off his list, Liam was leaning heavily toward Henry Lavender. He did have both motive and opportunity to have done it. Henry had freely admitted he'd wanted to break off his managerial relationship with Matty, but he wasn't having it. There was even a lawsuit involved. Certainly there had to be some animosity between Henry and Matty then? That was a strong enough motive right there. Henry now looked to be Liam's most probable culprit. Especially when you added in the note he'd found in Henry's room when he'd searched it. Despite Henry's protestations of not knowing where it came from he became Liam's main suspect. Liam just need some more proof to make an arrest

There was a commotion at the entrance of the Atrium when five additional uniformed cops from Liam's precinct arrived. This caused him to leave the pit to set them to their task of searching all the now opened rooms in the bathhouse.

Liam's exit also afforded Len and Dimity an opportunity to defy the detective again and seek out another clue to Benny's killer. The two of them left the pit and headed back to the hot tub room.

Len had been wondering how Benny's killer escaped the hot tub room to begin with? When they had all arrived Benny was the soul inhabitant found there, although by then Benny's own soul had also departed. His killer was long gone. So where had he disappeared too?

Dimity wasn't thrilled about going into the hot tub room again, not with the dead man still lying there beside the pool. For her his sheet covered body was too much like a Halloween goblin for her taste. "Can we move on, Len. It is creepy quiet in here."

"That's what we're here to do, luv. Move on. Anyway, I'm sure the coroner's men will be here soon." He spun around the room and then spied the door into the steam room. "That's the only way he could have gotten out of here. Let's go."

"Into there? I've never been in a men's steamroom before."

"Honey, there was a time when you weren't blond but you gave that a shot. Now come on."

Len opened the door and with a sweep of his hand escorted Dimity inside. The heat lay on her like a used beach towel at Coney Island. She swiped at her forehead. "It's absolutely oppressive in here. How can you guys stand it?"

"Hot is hot, dearie."

The room was empty. Just water slick tiled shelves for men to sit on and a thick mist swirling around making it difficult to see. She asked, "Where to now?"

Len pointed to the glass exit door on the other side of the room. Dimity was like a blind person as she groped through the fog toward it. She reached the door and pulled, letting a cloud of wet escape. Len was right behind her.

They found themselves standing in the shower area. Six silver spigot heads lined along one wall, each dripping water that ran to a drain at the center of the floor. At the far end of the space was a chrome rack piled with folded dry towels. A hamper bag inside a wire box stood next to that.

"So the killer had to have come through here, right?"

"I suppose he must have," Dimity mused. "But where did he go after that? We were all running by the outside door right after we heard the scream. We would have seen him, wouldn't we?"

Len shook his head. "I only saw Erik when we passed by. But he would have seen the guy while he was taking his own shower, right?" Len screwed his face into a question. "Maybe the killer hid in the steam room until after we all went to the hot tub area? Could that be it?"

"That would be for Erik to tell us. We need to ask him."

Dimity started to leave to go back to the pit.

"Wait a second. The killer would have had to clean up after hitting Benny, right? There had to have been some blood spatter on him from blows that severe."

Len went over to the hamper and started pulling out the discarded towels inside it. He threw them onto the floor in a pile until he gave out with an "Ah, ha." He held up a damp towel with smears of brownish red scattered across it. "Look at this. The killer must have wiped off Benny's blood and then stuffed it in here to hide it."

"And that's evidence..." Liam said from the doorway. "Hand it over. I'll need my lab boys to see that." He held out a hand. "And you two are pushing my patience to its limit. Both of your asses belong back in the pit." He held out an arm and pointed like a traffic warden. "Get! Both of you!" His voice had risen so he sounded much like Mrs. Hultz, Len's third grade teacher

They slunk past the pissed off cop and headed for the pit.

He huffed and followed them.

# XXIX

iam was talking to Henry and Erik, who were still sitting together on one of the steps in the pit. "All right, where the hell did he get off to? Where has JB gone?" Len and Dimity joined the two men as Henry, in answer to the detective's question, pointed toward the office. "He went that way."

Liam turned toward the staircase, put his hand to his mouth, and shouted, "Briggs!" His voice hit a decimal close to an air raid sirens wail.

One of the uniformed officers came out of one of the rooms upstairs and stood at the top of the stairs. "Yes, sir," he said.

"Get your ass down here," Liam yelled back. He waved a hand to punctuate his command.

The cop ran down to stand with him.

Liam stabbed at the cop's chest with a finger. "I want you to watch these people," he ordered, indicating the group seated in the pit. "If any of them make a move to leave I expect you to shoot them. Got it?"

"Yes, sir." Then as Liam was starting to move toward

the office, he asked, "You don't really want them shot, do you?"

"I want them here when I get back. Do what you need to do."

Len, sitting with the rest of the group, didn't think the cop watching them would really shoot at them, so he stood and went over to the piano. After all, he figured he was still in the pit so he shouldn't be fired upon. He sat down on the stool and took up a sheet of Henry's music from the holder.

Using the stub of a pencil he found in the grooves of the music rack he began to write on the back of the paper. He was taking JB's earlier suggestion. He'd come up with an idea for an ending to Henry's musical that was a lollapalooza. While contemplating Benny the Brit's murder he'd also managed to dredge up a fabulous idea for how *The Drag* could be closed. That "leap tall buildings" mind of his at work again. He had a finale to stun the audience to raucous applause. He was seeing trumpets and stairs, harps and choirs, as the now deceased drag of the title made her way to heaven in a white flowing gown studded with sparkles and spangles that glittered in the celestial lights. He wrote feverishly, getting the words of his beautiful inspiration down.

"Did I not tell you to stay..."

JB held up a finger to quiet him. "Yes, sir, it is important," he said into the phone. "Very important."

Liam, flummoxed a bit by that finger in his face, sputtered and took a moment to decide if he should just punch JB in the kisser or ignore his rudeness. He decided to ignore it.

JB, not even realizing he'd done anything, held out the phone at Liam. "Will you please talk to this man, Detective? You have to convince him to give us the information we need. Go on..." He pushed the receiver into Liam's hand.

Liam took the phone. "And who am I talking to?"

JB answered, "Matty Silverman's doctor. He refuses to tell me why Matty was at his office the day before yesterday. He's claiming doctor-patient confidentiality."

"Oh, he is is he? We'll see about that." Liam spoke into the phone. "Now see here, Doc." He didn't get any farther. Instead he was stuck listening to the doctor give him a lecture that ranged from whether he was really a cop or just a voice on the phone to the privacy between a physician and his patient to passages from the Hippocratic oath. Liam could only manage an occasional "Uh-uh" for his side of the conversation.

Finally, taking advantage when the doctor stopped to take a breath, Liam was able to get a word in. "Now listen here, bub..." He then strongly went on to advise him that he was indeed a detective and if he needed to verify that his badge number was seven, six, four, three. That information led to more listening for Liam on the proper way to address a physician and when and how it should be done. The doctor was obviously not a fan of the police.

At another break in the doctor's tirade Liam jumped in with his own. He'd had just about enough of this physician and his attitude toward the police. "Uh, excuse me, *Doctor...*"—with an emphasis on the sarcasm—"... but since the patient you seem so intent on protecting is the victim in an ongoing murder investigation the issue of confidentiality would seem to be moot. Isn't that so? The way I see this situation working out is this. You have three choices. You can tell us what we need right now on the phone. You can wait for us to get a judge to issue a warrant while you spend the rest of the day down at my station. Or, I can burst into your office with a squad of my officers and we can take your files out in front of your entire waiting room. Which would you prefer?" There was a silence, then Liam said, "I thought so." Liam looked over at JB. "Now, what was it we needed to know from the good doctor?"

JB said, "Simple. Why did Matty Silverman go to see him the day before yesterday? Was he there for himself or for his lover?"

"That's all you need?"

JB nodded.

Liam repeated the question into the phone.

"Uh-uh...Yes...All right. I understand." Liam looked at JB again. "There's nothing else?"

JB shook his head no.

"Then thank you, Doctor. You've been so very helpful." He handed the phone back to JB.

"Well, what did he say?"

"Mr. Silverman was there for two reasons. He wanted a prognosis for his lover, Gunnar, and..."

"And?"

"He was given the results of his own HIV test."

"And?"

"He was found to be positive. He had AIDS."

"Oh, God."

"Which fits with what I found when I searched Henry's room."

"What was that?"

Liam reached into his suit breast pocket and pulled out the folded piece of paper he'd found under Henry's mattress. He handed it over to JB. "That's looks to be Silverman's suicide note."

JB opened it and read it through. "It appears to be signed by Matty, true, but I see a couple of problems." JB held up the note facing Liam. "This note is typed. I would never trust a suicide note that isn't hand-written. Anyone could have done this."

"But why would they?"

"Maybe to throw blame onto an innocent party?"

"But that signature is his, JB. I checked it against his notebook."

"Really? Okay, but why is it so formal then? It's his full name. To his partner? His lover? His..what did he call him? His kinderstrudle."

"They may have had a more formal relationship than most. We don't know. Mary Todd didn't call her husband Abe she called him Mr. Lincoln."

"That was another century, and that marriage wasn't exactly made of sugar and marzipan. I read she insisted she be called Mrs. President by everyone. Pretentious much? Nuh huh, from all indications, Matty and Gunnar were happy together."

"Like I said, we don't really know. What we do know is there's a note with his name on it that indicates he could have taken his own life."

"All right, I'll give you that. It does look that way. And it goes a long way toward explaining the pose Matty's hand was in when we found him? If he'd been holding this note it would fit. And you say Henry had it?"

Liam nodded. "He swears he doesn't know how the note got into his room. But it was stuffed under his mattress. Remember, JB, Henry was found with the body, and he had a gun in his hand. I have to think he could have done it."

# XXX

The two men were walking back to the pit when Liam's sergeant came up to them. On Liam's orders he'd left his station in the lobby and had been searching one of the downstairs rooms. Now, draped over his arm was a long overcoat, and in his hand he held a man's felt fedora.

"Detective, I found these in there…" He pointed to the room at the side of the bar. Then added, "The other clothes in the room all belong to a woman. So the room was used by a real woman or a drag queen. Which one it might be is anybody's guess around here." He made a derisive sound.

Liam took the coat and hat from the cop and rather brusquely told him, "That'll be all. And you'd better watch that bigotry shit around me, Sergeant. I know its expected at the station, but I won't put up with it. Now go upstairs and continue looking there."

The sergeant gave the detective a look of pure anger at the dressing down he'd just been given. JB could see the beginnings of a temper tantrum starting to rise in him. It raged for only a moment though as the cop wisely stamped it down and stomped off toward the stairs.

That's interesting, JB thought to himself while watching the uniformed cop go off. Why the angry display of temperament from the sergeant? Were the detective and the officer an item of some sort? Humm, if so, that means the detective isn't available for pursuing after all? Well, that sucks big ass doesn't it? But if Liam is otherwise engaged he hasn't been acting like it most of the night. JB knew a flirt when he received one. If Liam is with someone there won't be any dating him, that's for sure. JB had a strict rule to not date unavailable men. Sure, he might crush on one of them if some of his past affairette's were any indication—a single roll in the hay was usually quite enough thank you—but he wouldn't keep pursuing them ad infinitum. It always got just too sticky. Jezz, that really does suck, he concluded. He'd been quite interested in the good-looking cop.

Oh well, he decided, he'd have to pull a Scarlett O'Hara over it and think about it another day. Right now the coat and hat the sergeant had delivered were what interested him the most. He said to Liam, "That's Dimity's dressing room over there, isn't it?"

"I think it is."

JB took the coat from Liam and held it up. "You know? If Dimity was wearing this coat and had that hat pulled down low over her face she would have been perfectly able to wander around the halls of this place without being detected as a woman. Anyone would have thought she was just another patron on his way to his room. And she did have that argument with Matty earlier in the evening. That's a motive isn't it? Could she have been angry enough to hurt the guy?"

"Are you insinuating that she might have done it?"

"I'm just saying."

"Well, we'll ask her. They're all in the pit waiting on us anyway."

JB and Liam didn't make it to the pit before Len and Dimity stopped them. Dimity spoke first. "We have something to show you that's puzzling us, Detective."

"Actually, so do we. But you go first."

She held out her hand. In it was the watch they had found in the hot tub. "It's Matty's, Detective."

Len said, "That was in the water where Benny's body was found. How it got there we don't know."

Liam took the watch, and shook his head. "This is getting curiouser and curiouser. What do you make of this, JB?"

"I think it means that Benny and Matty were entwined somehow."

"That's what I said, JB," Len offered. "But I can't figure out how. It's obvious that Benny was probably holding the watch when he fell in the water. But why? What did he have to do with Matty being killed?"

"And it gets even stranger, Len. It turns out Matty wasn't murdered after all. It looks more and more like he committed suicide. With pills. And there was a note left behind."

"And then somebody went in and shot him? After he'd taken a bunch of pills? Why?"

Liam said, "And that's the Twenty-five Thousand Dollar Pyramid question here tonight. Where's Dick Clark when you need him?"

JB shook his head. "You're absolutely right, Detective. The pieces of this puzzle aren't going together the way they should. It's damned frustrating."

Liam made a circle with his hand that encompassed Henry, Erik and Dimity. He said to them, "I know it was one of you three." There was a couple of gasps and a general denial from them all.

"So you suspect the diva, the piano player, or the back-up singer..."

"Add the words 'walk into a bar' and you have the makings of a great old joke." Len was putting in his two cents again.

JB gave him a look. Len shook his head. JB had at least twenty different ways of rolling his eyes and every one of them had a different meaning. The eye roll he'd just been given meant keep your nose out of it. He took a step back.

Liam went on. "What I'm having trouble with is pinpointing which of you it might be. So, I'll just ask outright. Was it you Dimity? Did you shoot Matty Silverman?"

She was shocked at the charge. She blustered, "No, of course not. I couldn't have done it. How could I have gotten up to his room?"

"Maybe we can clear that up right now?" Liam took the coat from JB and held it up. "Ms. London, is this your coat?"

JB added, "And is this your hat?" He held that up for her to see as well.

"Sure it is. But they're props. For a bit I'm working on for the act. I'm planning a Jimmy Durante tribute." She took the hat from JB and held it to her head, struck a pose, and lowered her voice to a masculine pitch. "Foist I'm gonna sing *Young At Heart* and then I'll use Jimmy's catchphrase." She imitated the big schnozzed, raspy voiced comic by saying, "Goodnight, Mrs. Calabash, wherever you are."

"Got it, Ms. London." Liam handed to coat back to JB. "And it explains why that coat was in your room. Right, JB?"

"Or it gives her a convenient excuse for having it."

Len shook his head. "The man doesn't know how to capitulate. Give it up, JB. She didn't do it."

"Okay, maybe you're right. This time."

# XXXI

tanding together, JB and Liam were still at the top of the pit. Len and Dimity had both moved down and were now sitting alongside Erik. Henry was hunkered over the piano keys picking out a tune with a single finger. Liam held out the watch Dimity had given him. "JB, take a look at this. There's something engraved on the back of it."

JB inspected it.

On the back casing, along with the manufacturing marks of a foreign company was a single word engraved in an Old English style script. Five letters that must have meant something to its owner. The word, however, wasn't in English. It was in some other language. It spelled *Älska*.

"Does that word mean anything to you, JB?"

"Nope. But it looks familiar. Where have I seen it? That accent over the A gives it a European origin."

"Matty Silverman had a foreign lover didn't he? Then the watch was probably his."

"Actually, I know it was Matty's. I saw him wearing

it when we spoke. Before he died. I recognize the band. And I have an idea where I've seen this word before. Do you have Matty's suicide note?"

Liam reached into his pocket and pulled out the paper. JB opened it quickly, scanned it, then put a finger on a word. "That's the same word, isn't it? Matty used it in his note."

"Who could we ask to translate this word?"

"Maybe Dimity would know what it means? She said she'd seen Matty wearing the watch too. It can't hurt to ask her."

Liam stepped down into the pit and called to her. When she joined them Liam handed her the watch.

"I already told you it was Matty's. He got it from Gunnar as an anniversary gift a couple of years ago."

"And the word on the back?"

She turned the watch over. "No idea. But Gunnar is Swedish, so the word is probably something in that language. Maybe Erik would know. Gunnar is his uncle after all."

JB spoke then, asking another question of Dimity. "Now that we know for sure that Matty did commit suicide, do you have any idea why he might have done it?"

She pondered a moment. "Well, now that I think about it, Matty had turned away from us the last couple of days. I didn't get it but he was real quiet... introspective, you know?"

JB nodded his understanding. He had seen it happen before with other friends of his who were dying. Just when you would expect them to turn to their friends for comfort and solace, instead they would go inside themselves to settle old hurts and grudges alone. JB had reached the conclusion that in the end death is a private thing between you and your beliefs. You end up praying to yourself for yourself.

Dimity went on. "Matty was down lately, but I figured it was because of Gunnar being so sick. That would get to anyone. Big time. But really, what purpose does it serve to ask why he'd do something like that to himself? It's a question that has no answer."

Liam corroborated what she said and added, "When you throw in that Silverman had just found out he was sick himself. It's a very compelling theory when you put it all together. Dimity, thank you for your help. You can sit back down now."

She nodded and went back to where Len and Erik were sitting on the steps.

JB, acting as if he was the tortoise in the famous fable—being slow to agree—asked Liam. "Did the doctor give you any indication of what Gunnar's prognosis was? What were his chances?"

Liam shook his head no. "Basically slim to none was my impression."

"But there was a chance Gunnar could survive his illness? People have made some miraculous recoveries."

"That's a big maybe. What are you getting at?"

"Okay, I think one or two of the pieces of this tangle are finally beginning to fit. You said that Gunnar had a chance of living. Okay, a slim one, but a chance. Then with his own diagnosis of full blown AIDS Matty would have thought he had an even smaller chance than Gunnar to live very long. I've known people who were diagnosed with AIDS and were gone a week later. Matty must have known that. All gay men do. He would have wanted Gunnar to be taken care of, wouldn't he? Are you with me so far?"

Liam nodded.

"Well, the money in his insurance policy would do that, right? Maybe Matty wanted to be sure Gunnar would be taken care of. Two hundred thousand dollars would go a long way. I think Matty decided he needed to die first. That way Gunnar would get his settlement. It makes sense in a woefully sad sort of way."

"But don't insurance policies have suicide clauses? If the policyholder kills himself the policy is then voided, isn't it?"

"That depends entirely on the individual policy. We can check. We have our own copy of it."

The two men went to the bar to read through Matty's paperwork again.

# XXXII

en was still in the pit sitting next to Erik on the tiled steps. Dimity, just returned from her conversation with the detective, sat down next to him. Len took a moment to consider what he and Dimity had discovered back there in the hot tub room. He tried for himself what he'd seen JB do at least a thousand times before. He took the facts he knew, laid them out in a logical order, and then extrapolated what the perpetrator's next steps might have been. If A had happened then B would be next, which led to C...

He turned to Erik and blurted, "I know what you did to Benny."

Erik, bored out of his skull was twiddling his thumbs and wool gathering. He sat up shock straight at Len's brazen statement. He was gobsmacked, as Benny would have said. "What was that?"

Len had put it out there with no preamble, as a blatant charge. Erik faced Len. "Say that again." His face had gone pale again. His eyes were popped like a 1930's cartoon figure.

"I said I know about you, Erik. Dimity and I found Benny's pictures of you. You make quite a lovely woman, my friend." Len held up one of the pictures he'd found in Benny's coat lining. "Although, I might have gone with a blond wig. That red hair really doesn't suit your coloring. You're much more a summer than a fall."

Erik grabbed the picture from Len's hand and tore it into pieces.

Dimity held up the two other snapshots. "Nice try, sweetie, but we have more." He grabbed across Len for those, but Dimity moved quicker than he could grab, and slid out of his reach. He sat back, then angrily began to mount a protest to the accusation Len had thrown at him.

Len held up a hand and said, "Now, hold on a minute. This is the way I see this...and please do correct me if I'm wrong. Benny had these embarrassing photos of you wearing a rather fetching gown and high heels. And I'm sure you were mightily embarrassed by them. You wouldn't want these to surface and ruin your closeted little life, now would you? They probably would have caused no end of problems for you? After all, if the Wizard had a set of nude pictures of the Wicked Witch Dorothy wouldn't have had to go to all that trouble over the ruby slippers, now would she? I think Benny chose last night to confront you with these pictures. Maybe he tried a bit of the old blackmail on you? I wouldn't put it past him. But you didn't want to pay, so you and Benny argued, and when it got really heated, you grabbed his camera out of his hands and you smashed his head in with it. Over and over. Am I getting the gist of it, Erik? Is that what happened?"

Erik had become almost catatonic as Len laid out the facts as he'd figured them out. Erik was sitting still as statuary, staring at his hands. Unable to deny the accusation Erik simply shook his head. Seeing no way out of his predicament he simply admitted to it. In a low voice he said, "He took the watch as payment. It was my grandfathers. Presented to him by his wife. She'd even had the word 'Love' engraved on the back. It was a family heirloom. It was mine. It belonged to me."

Dimity leaned in and patted Erik on the knee. "Nobody cares if you like to dress up, Erik. You didn't have to kill because of it. You went too far, sweetheart."

While Len was playing out this allegation with Erik Liam and JB had returned from the bar. They moved down to where the group was seated.

Liam had finally reached his own conclusion on the solution to the case. He'd done his due diligence, looked at the facts as he understood them, and decided which of his suspects the culprit was. He was sure he knew who the guilty party was. Even if that person hadn't actually killed Matty Silverman with his gun then he'd disfigured and maimed his body. That was still a crime. It was his duty to arrest the man for it.

He went straight to where Henry was seated and took hold of his shoulder. He stood him up, and turning him took out his cuffs to shackle him. He began by rote to repeat the Miranda warning—"Henry Lavender, I am arresting you for the mutilation and desecration of a dead body. You have the right to remain..."

JB, surprised at Liam's move, shouted, "Wait. What are you doing? You're wrong, Detective. You've got it all wrong. Henry didn't do it."

"Didn't he? I think he did. He had opportunity. He was found in the dead man's room. He took the suicide note. And he had the gun..."

JB couldn't let the detective carry out such a flagrant miscarriage of justice. "No, no. Sure, Henry was found knocked out in the room of the dead man. The person who'd actually done it knocked him out. And that note was planted in Henry's room to throw you off of the track of the real person who did it. And that gun Henry had? That little pea shooter wouldn't have done anywhere near the kind of damage that happened to Matty. His face was utterly destroyed."

"Uh, JB..." Len, who was now standing with his hands raised above his head, was trying to get his attention. "I'll bet you this gun here would have done that kind of damage. Don't you think so?"

Standing and facing Len and Dimity with a weapon in his hands, Erik was holding them at bay. He held on them what was essentially a short barreled shotgun with a hand grip. A blunderbuss. A virtual cannon. The weapon used shot instead of bullet's—steel pellets that could easily put a hole the size of a howitzer blast into its intended victim.

"And I know how to use this," Erik said. He stepped back to get a better aim at all of them.

Liam reached for his own weapon. He stammered. "Hey...what the hell?"

"No way, Detective. I want you to throw your gun over here. At my feet." Erik gestured with his own gun to enforce his threat.

JB said, "See. I told you Henry didn't do it. That's your culprit. It was Erik."

"It's too bad you couldn't have come up with that information a few minutes earlier." Liam put his gun on the floor and slid it over to where Erik was standing.

Len told JB, "He killed Benny too. Benny was trying to blackmail him. And Erik smashed his head in for it. Didn't you, Erik?"

"So what if I did?"

JB was surprised how easily Len had gotten Erik to confess to the killing of his victim. He would have to reassess his opinion of Len after all.

Dimity put another piece of the puzzle in place. "That's why Benny had Matty's watch? Erik used it to pay Benny off for these." She held out the pictures of Erik in drag.

Erik confessed a bit more. "I didn't have time to get the watch back from him. I had to leave it behind. You were all coming to crowd into the hot tub room. That watch was my grandfathers. Then Gunnar turned around and gave it to Matty. He shouldn't have done that. It was supposed to be mine. I wanted it."

JB asked, "So why did you shoot Matty, Erik? He was dead anyway. He'd taken an overdose of pills."

"The money, of course. It wouldn't have gone to Gunnar if Matty killed himself. The suicide clause in his policy. I had to make it look like a murder."

"You've been designated as Gunnar's beneficiary, right? When Gunnar died you would have got the two hundred thousand dollars."

"But, Erik, you don't get it," Liam said. "That wasn't the case at all. Matty's policy didn't have a suicide clause. The money would have gone to Gunnar no matter what the circumstances of Matty's death were. We checked. There's no such clause in the policy. Beside your shooting him wouldn't have covered up his drug overdose anyway. Since Matty died in an unnatural state..."

Len said, "Hey, is that another gay slur?"

JB sputtered and held in a laugh.

Liam looked at him oddly. "What? What did I say?"

"No, nothing. I'm sorry. Just a joke between Len and I."

With a look at Len that questioned the appropriateness of what he'd said, Liam went on. "Because Matty died in a public place the law requires that an autopsy must be performed. That would have discovered the barbiturates in his system. So you weren't covering up anything."

Dimity threw up her hands. "What a damn idiot you are, Erik. You fucked up, that's what you did."

Len looked at her. "Do you think its a good idea to insult the man holding a gun, hon?"

She snorted. "So says the kettle to the pot."

"Shut the hell up all of you..." Erik shouted, swinging his gun back and forth between Liam and JB, Dimity and Len. He knew they were trying to distract him, to gain some advantage on him. Now they were telling him he would have been caught no matter what. Goddamn it, life is really full of shit. Well, he wasn't going to let them get away with snowing him. "Then I'm in the clear aren't I? I can't be charged for shooting a dead man, can I?"

Len said, "Maybe for attempted murder?"

"No, not even that, Len. The law is pretty clear. The attempted murder of a dead body isn't a crime."

Liam had had enough. "But the mutilation and

desecration of a body certainly is. You're not going to pull this off, Erik..."

"All I want is out of here. I bet I can do that."

"I don't think so." Liam pointed upwards to the balcony above him.

It was lined with the six cops who had been searching the rooms above. Each of them had their service revolver targeted on Erik standing in the pit below them.

Dimity stepped forward and reached out to him. "Erik, honey, you can't do this. We're family. We all love you. You don't want to hurt anyone else, Erik. Come on, give me the gun, sweetheart..."

She reached out and grabbed hold of the barrel of the imposing weapon. Erik pulled back, away from her, struggling to loosen her grip on the gun. But she was a big girl and managed to hold on. She stepped in closer to strengthen her grip. The two grunted and grappled and pulled the gun back and forth between them like they were in a tug-a-war at a Sunday social. As they continued to wrestle Dimity somehow managed to twist the gun away from herself so that it was facing Erik.

The gun going off was a deafening explosion that shattered the bathhouse silence, echoing, bouncing, reverberating off the tile walls of the cavernous room. A sound loud enough that the onlookers covered their ears from the shrill heat of the blast. Erik gave out a shocked convulsive yelp, stood shock still, and then crumpled to the floor. There was a hole opening up his gut. A hole wide enough to spill his innards out onto his hands as they clutched at his bleeding belly.

Dimity scooted back, away from his body, her hands raised to her face. She cried, "Oh, my God, noooo." And then sunk to her knees, sobbing at the senselessness of what had happened.

# XXXIII

The paramedics lifted the wounded Erik to lay him on their gurney. He wasn't dead, but he had suffered a severe wound to his stomach, intestines, liver, and the adjacent internal organs. If the wound wasn't treated post haste it could see him dead within the hour according to the attending medics. They had seen to his immediate distress by staunching the worst of his bleeding and giving him a shot of a strong painkiller.

They moved to each end of the portable bed and lifted so they could carry him out of the pit and then roll him to the ambulance waiting outside. The lifting action caused him to moan as it shifted his body on the hard palette of the gurney.

JB was standing just over to the side, watching the medics as they made their way up the steps of the pit. Len, who'd been sitting on one of the tile steps gathering himself after witnessing the damage Dimity had inflicted, stood and came to stand beside him.

He started to speak, but JB wasn't paying any attention to what he was saying. He was more focused on the top of the pit and a little scene that was playing out up there.

The gurney had crested the enclosure, leveled, and was ready to roll to the outside when Dimity stepped up beside it. She took one of Erik's hands in her own, ostensibly to comfort him—at least that's what JB had thought was going to happen.

Even if he wasn't all that practiced in lip reading he could make out some of the words passing between the two. He got that Dimity said she was sorry to Erik. Then Erik, seemingly more concerned with her feelings than his own, answered her with a "No, it's okay." He began to pat her hand sympathetically.

What? Wait? The woman had just wounded him enough to put his life in jeopardy and *he's* comforting *her*? What the hell?

The medics went ahead and pushed past Dimity in their rush to get Erik his needed care. That left her standing alone looking after him as he was rolled away.

And within a second she had shaken it off. She managed to recover herself completely and no longer seemed the least anxious about her wounded friend. She raked a hand through her hair and then wandered over to the bar where she blithely ordered a drink from Brian the bartender.

Gears were meshing into action in JB's head as he watched this scene being played out. What wasn't right here? Again, there's something that doesn't fit. Was it Erik being more concerned about Dimity than himself? Or that once out of sight Dimity's own concern for Erik simply vanished? Whatever it was there was something very hinky going on here.

JB realized there was a buzzing going on beside him. Some mildly irritating noise that kept trying to intrude on his thinking. It was like the nagging of a child. Or a puppy whining. What was it? He focused in on the sound. It was Len prattling on about some such or other.

"What were you saying, Len? I wasn't listening."

"I was saying that I've done it."

"What have you done?"

"The ending..."

"What ending?"

"For Henry's play. Like you suggested. I wrote an ending for it. Have you heard anything I've said to you tonight?"

"I have had a couple of other things on my mind."

"Well, that's all finished and over with isn't it?"

"I'm not so sure."

"But we have both Benny's killer and the culprit in the mutilation of Matty Silverman. It's a two-fer. What else is there?"

"That's what I'm not so sure about. I have this odd feeling that this isn't over yet. There's some loose ends wandering about completely unresolved."

"Oh, that's just about you and that detective fellow. You do need to do something about him, you know? Ask him out why don't you? You are interested in him, aren't you? And it looks like he's free of any entanglements of his own."

"You think? I'm not so sure. But he isn't what's bothering me. However, you are right, I do need to talk to him about something."

"Well there you go. Now, about my ending."

"Sure, give it here. I'll take a look at it when I can."

Len handed over the scrap of paper he'd written his prose on. "Be careful with that. It's my only copy."

"And its pure gold I'm sure."

"Maybe just an alloy. It is only a first draft."

"I'll keep that in mind. Now where is that detective?" JB looked over at the bar and didn't see him, so he turned back to Len, "I'm going to go look for him. You stay here. Okay?"

He started to climb up the steps of the pit.

Len didn't do as JB asked. Instead of staying in the pit he headed over to the bar. As much as he would have liked to forget it he had an important errand to do there. He had to have that talk with Brian the bartender.

He was alone behind the bar, Dimity having wandered off somewhere of her own. Len went up and sat on one of the stools. Brian came over, and wiping the section in front of Len with a damp towel, he asked, "What can I do you for?"

"Brian, I need to talk with you about what you said earlier. About the audition."

Brian leaned against the back bar. "What? I let you off the hook and now you want to climb back on it."

"It's just that you are misinterpreting what actually happened back then. There's a bit more to the story."

His eyebrows lowered into a question. "And what would that be?"

Len gulped. This was going to be harder than he'd imagined. "Well, you said you had seven auditions for the part, right?" Brian nodded. "I had nine. For number eight I read with the leading lady, and for number nine I read for the network brass. After that I was offered the part. It turned out it wasn't you against me that was the problem. It was one type against another. A Heathcliff verses Mr. Darcy situation for the casting people. You were the Heathcliff type, the rough around the edges dangerous lead and I was the Mr. Darcy, the upper class aristocrat type. You and I were neck and neck all through the process."

"And they decided to go with you. I got that choice."

Len gathered his wits. "That's the misunderstanding I was talking about." Len gulped. In for a penny, as they say. Well, here's the pound. "They only decided to go with me when they were told you refused to audition anymore." Brian stood up straight ready to protest. Len went on before he could. "Maxine told them you had a better part to go to. You were taking that instead of doing their television show."

"But that isn't true. I'd have paid them for that part. The network made the decision to go with you. At least that's what Maxine told me."

Maxine had been their agent. She was the daughter of a well-remembered comic of the 1950's who had tried to make it as an actress on her own and found that she could represent actors better than she could do it herself. The old teach when you can't do it thing. She was also a horny old broad with a libido that was legendary. Her office casting couch was covered in clear plastic so it could easily be wiped down with Windex.

"Brian, you remember how aggressive Maxine was. I mean give the woman a pair of thigh high boots and a glue gun and she'd take you on a trip around the world. She wanted to get into my pants from the day I signed on with her."

Brian sniffed. "Sure, I remember. She was like that with me too."

"My sexuality back then could be called more fluid that it is now. I bedded both men and women along the way. When that part came along I..."

"You succumbed to her casting couch, didn't you? You slept with Maxine. You dog."

Len looked down at the bar. In a voice filled with the regret that had followed him over the years he said, "I did it to get that part. I screwed her on the condition that Maxine would stop sending you to the auditions. So I wouldn't have the competition. I'm the reason your acting career went into the toilet, Brian. And I am so very sorry."

Brian was still for a moment. Len braced himself for whatever might be coming. An angry tirade, a beating— then Brian laughed

"My own sexuality was pretty well set in stone by then. Maxine came on to me too, Len. But nothing was going to happen between us. Hell, she hit on every man she represented. Rumor had it she did the women too. I told her I wasn't interested. No, what happened to me wasn't really your fault. I did it to myself. Maybe if I had bedded her it would have been different. Maxine punished me for it too. Do you know where she sent me? To a season of Shakespearean repertory in Parsippany, New Jersey. I played Rosencrantz the gravedigger..." He snorted. "...which with this piece of information has some irony to it. I dug my own career a six foot hole eight shows a week." Brian tapped a finger on the bar. "But I should also add that it was out there in the

Jersey boonies that I met my lover. We've been together nine and a half years now. And I wouldn't have changed a thing, Len. My boyfriend owns this place. These baths are ours, plus we have a discotheque over in Queens, and a gay bar in Brooklyn. We're doing great. And in a sense I guess I have you to thank for it. If you hadn't screwed Maxine all of this would have never happened."

"She was the one of the last woman I ever slept with."

"I can understand why. A gay man with a woman is sort of like a vegetarian eating a steak dinner."

"Then you and I are okay?"

"Len, we both ended up with what we wanted. Of course we're all right."

Len took a breath. Well, that wasn't anywhere near as bad as I thought it would be. If the rest of the amends I have to make go as smoothly I just might be okay with it. He smiled to himself. And what a load off it is. I actually feel good. Like an albatross has left my back and flown off in search of another soul to torture. Do albatrosses fly, he wondered? Then he realized that he just might even be able to get some hours of consecutive sleep now. No more being tortured at four AM. Won't that be a change for the better. He yawned and stretched. You know what, he decided, this feels so good I think I might want to do it again. This is the same kind of rush I used to get when I was drinking. Back before I started counting my days. Then again, knowing me, I'll do what I usually do. I'll make amends after amends, again and again, becoming obsessive about getting that rush, until it finally gets so watered down it has no more effect for me. It will become just another routine and mundane exercise. Which will send me on a search for something else to get the rush back again. My addiction always plays these kinds of cruel games with me.

He stood from the bar and looked around. He was now alone. The lights of the back bar glinted off the bottles lined along its shelves My God, ain't they pretty. They called to him. Singing a familiar tune...Uh oh, I think I need to call my sponsor.

# XXXIV

**S**tanding at the top of the pit JB looked around and realized the detective still wasn't anywhere within eyesight, so he decided he would head for the office. Even if Liam wasn't there JB figured he could use the bathhouse sound system to put out a call that was certain to get his attention.

When he got to the office the door was ajar. A quick peek inside told him it was empty—the clerk must have stepped away for a moment. He went over to the desk.

Sitting in a swivel chair he leaned into the systems microphone, flipped the on switch, and prepared to put out an all points bulletin for the missing detective.

But before he could say a word he felt a pair of hands grab roughly at his shoulders and roll his chair away from the desk. The next thing he knew he was pushed up against the wall, still sitting, face to face with the angry person of Liam's sergeant. What was his name? Oh, yeah. Roger.

"You son of a bitch," he growled at JB. "You've ruined my life."

Well, that's an overly dramatic statement, JB

was thinking. What the hell did I do? And that's exactly what he asked the obviously pissed cop.

"But, why, Officer? How could I have done anything to you? I mean I barely know you."

The sergeant was surely a tad out of control. It appeared there was some unresolved issue he was trying to deal with by barely curbing his more pugilistic impulses. JB could feel the held in fight of him. It rippled just below his surface.

JB was trying to keep his voice as reasonable as he could while searching for an answer as to why this cop was confronting him like this. After all this guy was a New York City police officer. The kind that carried a gun and a badge. The kind of cop that could royally screw up JB's life. Roger, it looked like, was the one with all the power in this situation. "Uh, are you sure you have the right person, sir?"

Roger glared at him and said, "We were doing fine until you came around. Now it's all fallen to pieces. You've finished us."

Now that would seem to be a clue to what this is all about. But who the hell is the "we" in this scenario? That would help to know. "Who, officer? Who's finished?"

"Us, of course. And I'm going to get even. You're coming with me." He held up his handcuffs and rattled them in JB's face. "I'm charging you with resisting arrest and assaulting a police officer. How do you think that's going to play with him?"

Him? Us? Well, that hasn't cleared anything up, has it? However, it did mean there's another someone involved here. Now who the hell could that be?

JB began to run the events of the evening back across his mind. Who? Who? Scenes flashed by, speeding along pathways, neurons crisscrossing around in his brain. And all he kept getting was spinning wheels and whirling colors. WHO? Damn it. JB became aware that this entire situation was getting serious enough that he couldn't think clearly. Anxiety fogged his brain. As far as he knew he hadn't done squat to this guy, and now he was going to be railroaded by a very angry cop. He could end up facing a bevy of bogus and false charges. And the cop could get away with it. JB knew he was facing a lose-lose situation here. Then, luckily, from some deep recess in his brain, he grabbed an idea of who the other person in Rogers deranged scenario might be.

"You're saying you and the detective are finished, aren't you?" JB was guessing that the stomping around and the bad attitude the Sergeant had been exhibiting most of the night was caused by the end of an affair that he and Detective Liam were involved in. In even the best of circumstances that sort of thing could get real sticky. When one of the participants wanted to finish it and the other one didn't.

If that was the case, then Liam must have wanted to end what he and the Sergeant had going between them? Humm. Now that's possible. But how JB was involved in their thing he wasn't at all sure about. It couldn't have been the innocent flirting he and Liam had played at all night, could it? It was obvious that the Sergeant thought it was. And now he had lost his cool completely, aiming his displaced anger at JB.

JB was also sensing, even with all his irate posturing, that Roger really only wanted to talk it out, to make some meaning out of it for himself. JB didn't need to do anything except let him talk, to vent. If he let him do that maybe he would escape the anger that had started all this. So that's what he did. He remained still and let Roger ramble on. Roger wasn't even focused on JB anymore. His words were all smashed together, using JB as his personal sounding board.

"He said he wanted to be with me, but not like that....So what the hell is *that*? That's what I want to know? I must matter to him or he wouldn't have said it, right? He wouldn't have said anything if I didn't matter to him some little bit. But now he wants me gone. Phiff. Like that." He snapped his finger. "Gone. Out of his life..." He nodded as the pain inside caused his face to screw into a mask of hurt.

JB almost felt sorry for his attacker. Was that the Stockholm syndrome he'd heard about? "I get it, Officer. Really. But this isn't the way to take care of this. Nothing good can come of it."

The sergeant almost bawled. "There's nothing worse than this."

JB shook his head. "Nothing isn't better or worse than anything else. Nothing is just...nothing."

By this time JB had a feeling he should be all right. He was in no real danger after all. Looking over the sergeant's shoulder he could see his friend Len standing in the doorway. Come to access the situation. Thanks to that left open microphone he had heard the predicament the sergeant had put JB in and come to his rescue.

"Officer," Len said. "Just what in the hell do you think you're doing?" He stepped into the room and went over to the desk. He flipped the microphone to off, then turned to face the sergeant, who was still leaning over JB. He took a few steps to grab hold of Rogers shoulders and aimed the troubled cop away from JB. He directed him to another chair beside the desk. Roger sat heavily and heaved a tired sigh. Len squatted in front of him.

"You know you have got to let this go, Officer. I was in a play once. One of those Southern Gothic Tennessee William's wannabe dramas. One of the lines I remember was..." Len fell into a thick Mississippi accent. "You can't keep no man that don't wanna be kept, honeychild." He snorted and then dropped the accent. "You just have to let him fly away so you can fly too." Len continued to talk the distraught sergeant back down to something approximating normal.

JB stood and went to the door. He turned back and using hand signals, indicated to Len he was going to find the detective. He left the two men to continue their therapy session. JB had decided that Liam really needed to know about this incident, although he couldn't figure out why the detective wasn't there in the office already.

# XXXV

iam was to be found sitting in a back corner booth of the bar with a pair of Walkman sound buds stuffed in his ears. These portable tape players were a recent invention that served to effectively isolate people from other people. Every person was on their own mixed tape island and mostly unaware of what was going on around them. Liam's music went a long way toward explaining why he hadn't come to the office. He hadn't even heard the sergeant go off the rails.

He was busy checking his notebook and going over the notes he'd taken throughout the night. A policeman's job is only half done when he has his perpetrator in custody. After a case is wrapped there is still a mountain of paperwork to face. Reports have to be done in triplicate. Some sense needed to be made out of the events of the case for the review board. There were hours to be spent crossing I's and dotting T's.

JB went up to the booth and asked, "Detective, I

was wondering if I could have some of your time?"

"Only if you'll finally start calling me Liam." He smiled. And JB was totally charmed by his grin. The man really did have the nicest smile. JB slid into the booth across from the cop.

"Well, sure, if you insist. What I was wondering... uh, Liam, was if you are completely satisfied with our result tonight? Does this case feel finished to you? Is there maybe a loose end or two? Is there something hanging around unfinished."

Liam sighed and put down his notebook. "Such as?"

"Well, for one thing we've only made a guess that Gunnar's beneficiary was Erik. If it turns out he isn't then the whole case against him will fall completely apart. Is your friend still at work at the insurance company?"

Liam checked the clock above the bar. It said 9:30 but bar clocks were always set a half hour fast so they could make last call and close on time. It was around 9AM. "I think so. It won't hurt to call him I suppose."

As they went off to the office together JB took the moment to tell Liam what had happened with his sergeant. He wasn't thrilled to be informing on a cop, but by attempting to railroad JB he was clearly abusing his position. That was wrong. And that violent streak he was dealing with made him too much of a loose cannon. What if some real crook he was arresting was treated the same way? The sergeant had to be held accountable for his actions.

"That's right. The last name is Norske...Sure, I'll wait." Liam said to JB, "He's checking the files."

JB nodded. While he waited he took a look at the paper Len had given him. His climactic scene for Henry's play. It wasn't much, a longish couple of paragraphs only meant to describe action. No lines, simply exposition. JB read it through, then he read it again.

Liam answered the voice in his ear. "Yeah? Oh, there's two?" He looked at JB, "He's found two people under that name that have policies with New York

Mutual. A Gunnar and an Erik."

"That would be them. Can he check the beneficiaries on each of their policies?"

"Hold on." Liam made the request, then started writing on a new page of his notebook. "Now that's interesting..."

"What did he say?" JB asked.

Liam tore the page out of his notebook to hand it to JB.

He looked it over. "I see what you mean..."

# XXXVI

hey found her in her dressing room packing a valise. Although calling it a dressing room was giving it more elegance than it really possessed. It was also a storage room holding wire shelves filled with bar supplies—napkins, swizzle sticks, jars of olives—plus twenty or so boxes of imported beer stacked against the wall.

"Where do you think you're going, Dimity?"

"I'm getting the hell out of here, bub. I've had it with this place. This gig is over. Kaput. Done. My back-up singer might die and my manager's already dead. There's nothing but bad mojo around here. I won't stay for it to get me too."

Liam had reached the point in the evening where he had little to no tolerance for any pussyfooting around. This case had taken one too many turns already and this latest was the end for him. He put his and JB's most recent discovery out into the room like TNT going off.

"But I'll bet you'll take the two hundred thousand dollars that Erik's insurance gives you, won't you? That is when he die's from his gunshot wound."

She stopped packing, standing like a piece of sculpture for a long moment. Then she sat heavily at her dressing table. Watching JB and Liam in the mirror she said, almost fluttering—as if she was some Falkner heroine—"Why, whatever do you mean?" She couldn't carry it off. It was Ernest Borgnine attempting to play Lady Windermere.

Liam and JB both began to pepper her with questions. Each throwing an accusation at her in turn.

"We checked with New York Mutual Insurance, Dimity," JB shot. "Erik had his insurance policy there along with his uncle."

"So?"

Liam pointed a finger. "It all follows a line, Dimity. From Matty to Gunnar to Erik...to you."

"But," JB added. "Like domino's falling, each one of them has to die for you to make your profit at the end."

"How did you get Erik to go along with your scheme, Dimity? Did you use blackmail the same as Benny tried to do?"

"You stepped in and got Erik shot in the gut on purpose, didn't you? That heroine thing, saving all of us from a crazed gunman, was just an act. A way to be rid of him so you'll get your payoff."

Dimity's face registered each piece of evidence they threw at her as if struck by a flying hardball, like the penny a pitch game at a Times Square arcade. She physically reacted to each accusation. Her breathing became ragged, each gasp building on the other. Her anger growing as she felt each verbal blow lobed at her. Finally she yelled. A gut wrenching cry at a pitch that hurt their ears. It went on and on. She began to slap her hands on the table in front of her. Pounding out her anger in a Morse code of frustration and temper.

"Are you guys nuts?" she screamed. She was trying to bluster her way out of the corner they had her trapped in.

She stood suddenly, and as she did she grabbed a

jar of cold cream from her dressing table. Going into a
pitchers stance she threw the jar in the general direction
of JB and Liam. They ducked as the projectile flew past
them to explode against the wall with a satisfying crash.
White goo slithered down the wall. Dimity yelled again
and stepped over to the wire shelves. If a jar of cold
cream would cower the men maybe more would afford
her an escape route. Her instinct was to flee. To get
away from her persecutors.

She grabbed what was at hand. Object after object,
boxes, jars, packages of napkins, swizzle sticks—all of
them were hurled willy-nilly at the two men. They were
left no other recourse but to crouch and cower from the
onslaught.

Her tirade still not done Dimity next went for the
boxes of beer. She ripped open one of them and began
hurling twelve ounce bottle's one after the other like
they were grenades. They crashed against the walls
sounding like an artillery barrage. Exploding one after
another, spewing liquid to drench the two men with
glass and brewed hops. The barrage forced them to
remain hunkered down by the door in fear of the glass
shards that showered over them.

Len and Henry were sitting together at the bar. They
heard the explosions coming from a distance and stood
up like prairie dogs in the desert at the sound. What
the hell was that? Another bang exploded. This one
was loud enough to locate the chaos as coming from
the dressing room at the side of the bar. Dimity's room.
They made their way there to investigate, crowding into
the entrance to see what was happening.

Their curiosity had essentially cut off any escape
Dimity might have tried. Her anger still not dissipated
she looked past Liam and JB to the doorway where
Henry and Len were standing. Foiled in her escape she
had no choice but to beg for some support.

"Henry," she screeched. "Say something, damn
it. You know this is pure bullshit. I had no idea that
I was to get any money. That Erik had made me his

beneficiary."

Henry wasn't having it. "Oh, give it up, Dimity." He had suffered through too many of these tantrums of hers. He was taking this one with less than a grain. He saw it as a spoiled girl acting out. A diva gambit she used to get her way. "You can't bluff your way out of this one. All of us could see how you managed to manipulate Erik into doing anything you wanted. Hell, your hand was so far up his butt you could make his lips move."

JB added, "You took the fact Erik was crazy about you and engineered this whole thing. You really are one very malicious bitch."

"No. I wouldn't do that. I'm a nice person. I really am."

The laughter from the men watching her took any wind that was left out of her tirade. Finally realizing that her anger was futile she gave up and dissolved into tears. Great racking sobs of self-pity making her whole body shake. Gasping and sobbing she stumbled to her dressing table and collapsed onto the stool. Through her sobs she moaned, "Do you have any idea how much it costs to build a career in this town? Singing classes, dance classes, photos, agents, on and on. Money spent and always more needed. But, I would never go that far. To wound Erik on purpose..."

JB scoffed, "Wicked is as wicked does, Dimity. Lesser. Greater. Middling. It makes no difference. The degree is unbending. You is what you is, dearie,"

Liam stepped over to the dressing table. "And you, Ms. Dimity London, are under arrest for aiding and abetting. I might throw in obstruction and fraud for good measure. Maybe depraved indifference too. If you'll come with me..."

He stood her up and led her to the door.

Henry and Len stepped aside to watch them exit.

JB, still in the room, said to them, "I'm glad you're both here. Come in. I want to talk with you."

They moved inside and sat on the couch facing JB.

"You read it, didn't you, JB?"

Henry asked, "Read what?"

"I wrote a possible new ending for your show. JB thought there was a problem with the main character killing himself, so he challenged me to write something that would circumvent the issue. And I did it, didn't I, JB?"

"Well, you did write an ending..."

"And you loved it."

"I wouldn't say that exactly. I have a few reservations."

"You do do you? God, you can be such a stick in the mud..."

"Now that I know for sure is a gay slur."

Len didn't laugh this time, instead he continued to look steadily at JB.

"Okay, Len, I read it." He sighed. "And then I read it again."

"And?"

"You do want the truth, right?" Len nodded. "Then here goes." JB took a breath, exhaled, then said, "After I read it I wanted to gouge out both my eyes and hide the scene up my ass so I'd never have to see it again." He paused a moment for Len to absorb what he'd said. "I'm sorry, sweetie."

"You didn't like it. Well, what do you know?"

"I know that you used every cliché that's been around since Shakespeare first took up a quill. This scene you've written is a straight-up rehash of Lil' Eva's death in *Uncle Tom's Cabin*. Including angels flapping their wings and choirs singing the ascent. And it was an old idea when Harriet Beecher Stowe used it in eighteen-fifty-two."

"I swear, JB, asking you for advice is like asking Donald Trump if he knows a good hairstylist."

"What you two need to do is find yourselves a writer who has some real élan. One who would go beyond the more obvious choice and come up with an ending that has some style and meaning." Len leaned forward to say something. JB held up his hand. "No. I have deadlines I have to meet. There's a first draft expected at my publishers."

"What sort of meaning are you talking about?"

Henry asked.

"Well, off the top of my head...How about if your drag hero was somehow the inspiration for the queens that started the riots at Stonewall? It's his spirit that gives those drag queens the courage to fight back for the first time. That's an idea..."

"And an interesting one. I could work with that. Sort of *Les Miz* meets *La Cagé*."

"There you go. Use it if you want. Len, you're a fine actor. An excellent interpreter of the words given you by others. But you ain't a writer of them. Please don't try."

"What about that book offer I got?"

"I'd say forget it. Writing your story should be like pirate's treasure. Buried on a deserted island."

# FIN

**I**t's been several weeks since the events of that night at the tubs, and, as time must always do, it has continued on. Since that night Len's predictions of closing notices on his Broadway show have proved true. Which has resulted in his focusing on *The Drag* as his next project. He's been working non-stop with Henry Lavender for their musical about Julian Eltinge, the impersonator of their title.

JB has even heard a couple of the songs and thinks they might be good. They are hummable at least.

They do still have problems with their libretto, but JB has managed to keep his opinions to himself—so far. JB had, just to amuse himself you understand, been coming up with a couple of fixes for Len's play.

His thought was they should open with Eltinge in the 1940's, when, by some draconian law, Los Angeles County wouldn't let Eltinge wear his own dresses in his nightclub act. He had to do his performance by standing at a rack of his costumes on hangers and describing to the audience what he would do in them.

Try telling anyone there isn't a musical number that

scene. That would be followed by a flashback to when Julian was on top of his game to continue the show.

Contending with a clothes rack of evening gowns would have to be something that Len needs to think hard about with this idea of his. Dressing in women's clothes eight times a week is going to cause some controversy along Broadway. So Len has actually decided now is the time for him to officially come out as a gay man. Newspaper articles, TV news coverage, the gay press, the whole schmear—he's angling for a piece in the *Sunday Times Magazine* section.

To be honest his being gay isn't really all that much of a secret to most anyone among the New York theater crowd. To them he's never been in. They all knew which side of the toast his butter is spread on. But he feels his coming out to the general public would help to generate publicity for the show. Furthermore, Len has, through his connection with ACT-UP, come to believe that being out—not living a lie, staying in a closet only long enough to hang up his coat—is the only way he will be able to keep going. These are dangerous times and the gay community is at the epicenter of a national debate. The more people that learn gay people exist everywhere might go a long way toward making them learn some tolerance.

JB has kept busy writing the next installment in his Bent Mystery saga. *Bullet's In The Bathhouse* has been a working title. Along with *Tubs And Guns,* or *Bathhouse Bloodbath!*.

If that last title wasn't quite so trashy it would certainly fit the cast of characters he's working with on this particular book. Plus it's a hoot to let the two words roll off your tongue. Try it, you'll like it.

JB has kept in touch with Liam Kelly, the homicide detective he met that night. They've been on four or five dates so far and interest is continuing to build between them. There was a strong connection that night at the baths, the last place JB ever expected to find a new boyfriend.

Roger, Liam's sergeant had quickly retired from the force after it was made clear he could be brought up on misconduct charges if he didn't.

Erik survived his wounds and will be going to trial in the next few months. Dimity will be testifying against him, having worked out a plea deal with the prosecutor's office.

JB and Liam could be said to be at the "I think maybe I'm in love with you, but I don't want to say it yet" phase. Basically really good boink buddies at this point. Liam has spent several nights at the apartment and had even been of some help as JB was working on his book. Liam was very good at jogging JB's memory —along with some of his other body parts too.

And that's all, folks.

# About the author:

Ken Lansdowne has lived in California, Nevada, New York City, New Mexico, and now lives in Denver Colorado.

The first novel in *The Bent Mystery* series is *Secrets Don't Belong In Closets*, the beginning. Second is *A Murderous Ball of Fluff. The Fairy Dust Killer* is the third. Fourth is *Home Sweet HoMo*. Fifth is *Dance:Ten Murder:Maybe?*. Sixth is *A Mystery, Wrapped In A Mystery, Surrounded By A Mystery*. Seventh is *The Art Of Death,* and number eight is *Bathhouse Bloodbath!*

There is also a Gay themed Christmas novella: *Jacob Marley*

If you would like to get an automatic e-mail when the next book in the series is ready for release sign up at k.lansd@outlook.com. Simply put the word "LIST" in the subject line of your email. Your e-mail address will never be shared and you can unsubscribe at any time.

Word-of-mouth is crucial for any author to succeed. If you enjoyed the book please consider leaving an online review, even if it is only a line or two: it would make all the difference and would be very much appreciated. If you didn't like it I apologize for taking up your time: my purpose was only to entertain or give you a laugh or two.

www.ingramcontent.com/pod-product-compliance
Lightning Source LLC
Chambersburg PA
CBHW070823120626
46556CB00002B/638